THE GREAT WITCHY CAKE-OFF

WONKY INN BOOK 7

JEANNIE WYCHERLEY

The Great Witchy Cake Off
Wonky Inn Book 7
by

JEANNIE WYCHERLEY

Sign up for Jeannie's newsletter: www.subscribepage.com/JeannieWycherleyWonky

The Great Witchy Cake Off was originally edited by Anna Bloom @ The Indie Hub (2019)

and Christine L Baker (2021)
Cover design by JC Clarke of The Graphics Shed.
Formatting by Tammy

Please note: This book is set in England in the United Kingdom.
It uses British English spellings and idioms.

The Great Witchy Cake Off is dedicated with love to all of those—contestants, judges, producers, technicians, runners and presenters—who have ever appeared on any television baking show both here in the UK and in the US.

I'm a total baking show junkie and I adore cake, so this story has been written with love, respect and my tongue planted firmly in my cheek.

But it is especially dedicated to Kim-Joy from GBBO 2018 because it was while I was watching her decorate her cakes using teeny tiny British wildlife characters that I first spawned the idea for this novel.

With grateful thanks
Jeannie Wycherley

CHAPTER ONE

"Alf? I've brought the post up." Charity leaned across the desk, holding a single letter out to me. I reached for it automatically, but something about the colour gave me pause. I took a closer look and snatched my hand back in revulsion. A fine quality stained parchment envelope. Cursive handwriting. A foreign stamp.

"Burn it." I curled my lip as Charity's hand continued to hover in the air between us.

A look of uncertainty crossed her pretty face. "Burn it?"

Folding my arms, I swung back in my chair, the spreadsheet on my computer screen all but forgotten. "I'd recognise that handwriting anywhere. And that absurd old-fashioned coffee-stained stationery." I frowned. "*Sabien*."

Charity's eyes widened and she carefully turned the envelope over to scrutinise the writing. "It's a French stamp," she agreed. "I think you're right."

I snorted. "I know I'm right. Burn it. Shred it. Feed it to Finbarr's pixies. Add it to the compost. Pour acid over it. Whatever. I really don't care. I just don't want to know what it says or what he wants."

Had it really been nearly twelve months since Whittle Inn had entertained several carriageloads of vampires? I'd been persuaded by Charity and, to be fair, my own stupidity, that opening my wonky inn whilst at the same time hosting a vampire wedding would make good financial sense. The entire event had rapidly turned into a nightmarish experience I had no desire to ever repeat. I usually considered myself a fairly egalitarian kind of witch, happy to accommodate anyone and everyone, whatever their particular flavour or magickal penchant. Even faeries.

But vampires were barred.

Forever.

No exceptions.

Charity opened her mouth to speak again, or maybe to protest that we should at least take a look at the contents of Sabien's missive, but her words were drowned out by the thunderous clanging of heavy metal poles dropping on top of each other on the lawn outside. The production crew for *The Great Witchy Cake Off* were erecting their enormous marquee, and it sounded like they'd had another delivery of supports. The noise set my teeth on edge and made my ears ring.

"How much longer?" I wailed. I jumped up and strode to the window, intending to pull it closed. But I'm naturally nosy, as I'd been reminded on many occasions, so instead I found myself hanging over the ledge, straining to see what the production crew were up to.

I'd never had much to do with the filming world before, apart from when the local news had been in the village to report on the Psychic Fayre the previous April. Now I found myself grudgingly entranced.

Okay, that's a lie. My entrancement wasn't *grudging* at all.

I was absolutely *dying* to see how they made a television programme.

The crew had arrived several days before with truckloads of equipment and resources. I had never imagined they would require so much. I'm fairly certain that getting the articulated lorries down some of our narrow local lanes would have been an adventure in itself.

Then they'd started to lay out a production village of sorts, with make-up trailers, an editing suite and storage for expensive technical equipment. Noisy generators had been placed out of the way around the side of the inn, and thick power lines ran into the area where the famous marquee would be raised. These black cables had to be covered with imitation grass to ensure they weren't visible to the naked eye during filming. Various tour buses and vans for the use of the production team and crew had been parked far back out of sight, almost within the hedgerow that made up the front boundary of the grounds of Whittle Inn.

It rapidly became apparent that to the production crew aesthetics were everything. This late in the season, we still had roses blooming in the gardens, along with some clematis plants, nerine, begonias and a few ivy-leaved cyclamen, but Ned and Zephaniah were beginning to prepare for the winter ahead by clearing some of the flower beds. *The Great Witchy Cake Off*'s producers had other ideas, however, and several flat-bed trucks had brought along dozens and dozens of bedding plants and bushes in pinks, whites and reds, and even a few statues to enhance what the gardens of Whittle Inn already offered.

To be fair, the garden had never looked so good. I had my fingers crossed that the producers would leave everything in situ when they departed, once filming had been completed of course.

The beautification hadn't stopped there. In addition to the garden improvements, the set design wizards had carefully repaired the scorch marks on the white walls of the inn; scars caused by the little skirmish I'd had with The Mori during the early part of the summer.

So far, I couldn't complain. The inn looked fantastic and would photograph well. With any luck, the publicity generated by hosting *The Great Witchy Cake Off*—one of the most popular baking programmes ever to air on Witchflix—would stand us in good stead and encourage a greater volume of bookings.

And anyway, who could fail to feel a little star-struck by the celebrity judges and presenters?

I'm happy to admit—as a deeply-hidden-in-the-closet fan of the show myself—that even I'm not immune to curiosity about how the other half lives. So you can imagine what sort of state Florence, my long-dead housekeeper, was in. The term 'excited' cannot possibly or adequately summarise her effervescent maelstrom of emotions. Although I'd tried to keep her calm, I'd failed, and now she flitted around the inn and the grounds at the speed of light, trying to be everywhere at once. Any time a camera operator pointed his expensive-looking gadget at a bush or a statue, Florence was there, smouldering happily and overseeing the shoot. When I say smouldering, you'll understand I don't mean in a sexy way at all. Florence had actually burned to death, and now her ghost continued to smoulder away for eternity. It could be quite disconcerting for anyone who came across her unexpectedly, but once you got to know her, you didn't let a small thing like her appearance put you off.

Unable to contain herself, Florence was everywhere at once. At any moment I expected one of the producers to either grumpily banish her—by exorcism no doubt, because unless you're a 'ghost whisperer' that's the only way you can get rid of ghosts—or haul me over the coals for allowing Florence free rein to disrupt their work.

But I kind of understood Florence's giddiness.

Just yesterday one of the two judges, Raoul Scurrysnood, had arrived in his silver Tesla Roadster with the top down. I'd found my legs propelling myself onto the gravel drive in front of the inn at a rate of knots, offering my hand—ostensibly for him to shake —then blushing furiously when he kissed it instead. Oh, the man was charming! Citrus-green eyes and beaming white smile. His silver hair, beard and moustache had all been freshly trimmed, and his clothes were immaculate; dark grey slacks with a crisp linen shirt.

Standing in front of him in stark contrast, I presented as a wildling with my unkempt hair, slightly shabby robes and no make-up. My own fault. I should have listened to my great-grandmother—also deceased—and made more of an effort.

Back in the present I heard Charity crumple Sabien's correspondence in one hard fist before coming to join me at the window. Below us, members of the crew worked efficiently to position poles under the canvas of the marquee. No messing around, no fuss, no drama. They carried on with the job in hand, each knowing what the others were doing and communicating in a happy and courteous way.

The same could not be said for the producers themselves.

To the left of us, part way down the drive, I could clearly make out the gorgeous Raoul standing with

The Great Witchy Cake Off's 'bosses'. These included Patty Cake, an infamous celebrity in the witching world who often sat in the front row at fashion shows and had graced the cover of *Witch in Vogue* several times, and Janice Tork-Mimosa, a quieter woman with an inordinate amount of class and her own dollop of glamour. They were joined by a tall, slender man with a neat Elizabethan-style moustache and beard, wearing a black crewneck jumper with a green silk paisley cravat. Behind him a single camera operator, a wizard of some kind judging by his robes, was getting in everyone's way and filming them as they milled about.

As we watched, a small red hatchback drew up and parked on the drive. An extremely short and round woman with grey hair pulled herself out and beamed at the producers.

I squinted. "Is that Mindi Blockweg?"

Charity leaned out further to get a better look and I grabbed hold of her in case she fell. "The main presenter? I don't know. Is it? She's smaller than I imagined."

"Everyone looks larger on the TV than they do in real life, apparently," I replied. "I've heard it adds ten pounds to you."

Charity giggled. "You'd better lay off the cake then, Alf."

I turned to stare at her, dropping my mouth open in mock shock. "Cheeky! I'm built for comfort, not speed." I patted my hips. "Besides, I'm not planning on making any unscheduled appearances on the programme."

"Wasn't your agent able to negotiate a high enough fee?" Charity asked, and I snorted.

I made light of it, but her words stung a little, and to be fair she was right. I'd lost a lot of weight while training with my dark witch friend, Horace T Silvanus—Silvan for short—earlier in the summer, but lately I'd put some of it back on.

"Ooh! Look. There's Faery Kerry," Charity exclaimed, her voice full of awe. Faery Kerry was a legend in her own lifetime. A petite old lady, as faeries tend to be of course, with delicate features, white hair and slightly pointed ears. Even from our vantage point at the window, we could feel the charisma emanating from her. She hugged the others, and an animated discussion followed as the camera wizard danced around the group and captured their reunion.

Figuring I'd seen all there was to see for now, I was about to return to my spreadsheet when raised voices drew our attention once more. Patty Cake, the more vociferous of the producers, appeared disgruntled about something.

"I'd better go down and find out what's up." I pulled away from the window. "Make sure you destroy that letter," I reminded Charity before fleeing down the stairs.

I rushed to join the gathered throng on the drive. As I pounded through the bar, I could hear them all talking loudly over each other. I arrived, breathless, just in time to hear Janice soothing Patty with the words, "I'm sure Alf, the owner of the inn, can handle it."

"What would you like me to handle?" I chirruped, plastering a big smile on my face while pretending not to notice Raoul's laser stare. He certainly had a way of making a woman feel weak at the knees. Faery Kerry and Mindi Blockweg stepped back, keeping a polite distance, obviously not wanting to be involved in any ugliness.

Janice smiled at me. Of the two producers, I would have thought she was the younger: a woman in her forties, her shoulder-length hair slightly greying at the temples and loosely curled. She dressed well—not cheaply, but not in an ostentatious way either. Today she was wearing a black dress with a bright red belt and matching lipstick. She'd thrown a black and white check scarf casually around her shoulders. If I looked as good at her age, I'd be happy. "Oh, Alf," she said sweetly, "we're sorry to bother you. It's just Patty is used to more space to work in and she's struggling with her bedroom allocation. She thinks that trying to work at the dressing table in her room is inhibiting her creativity."

I pulled a face in sympathy. Patty peered through her dark sunglasses at me. As skinny as Penelope Quigwell, they could almost have been sisters. Patty's jet-black hair was cut in a razor-sharp page boy, and in spite of the fact that she must have been in her sixties, there wasn't a white hair to be seen. A thick layer of foundation covered her wrinkles admirably. "I'm so sorry. I hadn't really thought about your need for an office in advance," I said. "If you like, I can have a desk and chair brought up to your room?" At the very least this would give the Wonky Inn Ghostly Clean-Up Crew something to do, rather than hang around watching the production crew doing all the work.

Janice's eyes crinkled in gratitude. "That's so kind—"

"Out of the question," Patty's deep modulated

voice chipped in. "The room is small enough as it is. I can't possibly squeeze any more furniture in."

My stomach performed a nervous little flutter. After much consideration I'd placed the judges, Raoul and Faery Kerry, in my largest rooms—*The Throne Room* and *Neverwhere*—and then the presenter, Mindi in the next sized room, *Stoker*. My thinking was that people loved to watch *Cake Off* for the personalities of the judges and presenters, and therefore they were the most valuable. I'd obviously not considered the producers as important as they undoubtedly were. An error on my part.

"I do apologise." Thinking quickly, I countered, "Why don't I clear The Snug on the ground floor? It's a little room behind the bar and you can use that as an office."

Once more Janice tried to interject, "That would be wonderful!" but Patty was faster.

"Honestly, darling. I have no idea to where you're referring, but I can't imagine that an office down one of your draughty little corridors will be particularly comfortable."

"I—" I started to protest but Patty held up a thin hand, her viciously pointed nails pointing up to the sky, and stopped me. "Don't worry, Wilf. I've made my own arrangements."

"It's Alf—"

"Alf? Wilf?" She genuinely looked confused. "What's the difference? It's a silly boy's name."

"Patty..." Janice chastised her co-producer, but only gently.

"Oh, do chill, Patty." The slender man with the tartan scarf fluttered his eyes at me, sounding bored. "I'm so sorry about this."

"Don't apologise on my behalf, Boo," Patty snapped. Boo Sully. That's who he was. The director. He waved his hands around gracefully and giggled, entirely unconcerned by Patty's histrionics. "I can't and won't stay here."

I clenched my jaw and persisted. "We have a fire in The Snug. I can make it cosy for you."

Patty turned the corners of her mouth up into the ghost of a smile. "No need to fuss, my darling. I've made alternative arrangements already."

Already?

"Raoul here has offered to give me a lift." Her hand flapped in Raoul's direction and when I looked his way, he raised his eyebrows. An invitation to something I didn't want to pursue.

"Patty?" Janice tried again. "You know we need you on site—"

Patty tutted. "I won't be far away. There's a

modern inn down in the quaint little village we passed through. It has much larger rooms and all the mod cons I need. I'll be very comfortable and just a quick drive away."

"The Hay Loft?" I asked, and my voice rumbled with a stony undercurrent I couldn't quite hide.

"Is that's what it's called, Wilf? How cute." With that, Patty swirled on her kitten heel and slunk away in the direction of Raoul's car.

Raoul's grin reminded me of a cheetah. "I won't be long," he told Janice. Winking at me, he followed Patty to his car. I stared after them in consternation.

Janice, seeing my expression, patted my arm. "Don't worry. I could have booked Patty into the Ritz and she'd have taken it as a personal affront. She does this every time, changes accommodation at least once, sometimes two or three times a shoot. It's nothing to do with you or your lovely old inn."

From behind us came the purr of the engine of Raoul's Tesla Roadster, followed by the scattering of gravel as he swiftly turned it about. "Well, we'd better hope she likes The Hay Loft," I chipped in, while actually hoping she loathed it. "Because besides them and us, the only places to stay in a five-mile radius would be tiny bed and breakfasts."

"Oh, I'm sure—"

Janice was rudely interrupted by the sound of a car skidding on gravel. Raoul had been attempting to speed down the drive—probably trying to impress us all with his car's nought-to-sixty capability—and had encountered a green and gold van lumbering towards us from the opposite direction. Given the narrow nature of the approach to the inn, the vehicles had almost careered into each other.

There was an angry exchange between the occupants of the Tesla and the driver of the van before the van edged almost into the hedge to allow the sports car to go on its way. At last Rob's Porky Perfection food wagon ambled towards us and pulled to a stop. I walked over to greet him.

"Hi Rob," I said as he leaned out of his window.

"Where would you like me?" he asked.

I indicated the edge of the gardens where the production trailers had been parked. "Along there, with those."

Janice joined us. "I'm sorry. What's this?" she asked.

"In the details you sent me, I was asked to provide catering for everyone. Naturally I have Monsieur Emietter and the inn's kitchen offering some top-notch cordon bleu, but I thought it would be fun to have Rob here too." Janice looked blank, and I realised the details had probably been forwarded to me on her behalf, by some member of the production crew or an admin assistant. Who could tell?

"But it's a burger van." Janice's voice rang with disdain.

Rob grunted in indignation. "It's not a burger van at all!"

It was my turn to pat Janice's arm reassuringly. "Sausages. And the quality is exceptional."

"Don't knock it till you've tried it," Rob called and slammed into gear, driving noisily away.

"All local products," I added, watching him roll across my lawn to the space I'd indicated. "Honestly Janice. Trust me. The crew will love his meals and it's all on the house." I'd arranged to pay Rob for his time and products, and it gave me an excuse to indulge my craving for sausage and mash.

"If you're sure," she said, casting a worried glance at Faery Kerry and Mindi.

"I am!" I trilled. "There'll be plenty of healthier choices from our own kitchen, so no worries on that score." Mindi smiled at me, obviously amused by the carry-on.

I warmed to her straight away. "I'm sorry," I said

to the newcomers, "I've been so rude. I'm Alfhild Daemonne. Welcome to Whittle Inn."

"Thrilled to be here," exclaimed Faery Kerry. "Such gorgeous countryside, but so far from civilisation."

"Indeed," drawled Mindi and indicated her battered little red Renault Clio. "T'was the very devil to find. Are you providing valet parking?"

I held an astounded laugh in check.

Valet parking for a 2004 Renault Clio? Draughty corridors? Bedrooms that were too small?

Who were these people?

The Great Witchy Cake Off had arrived in town, and I was beginning to wonder what I'd let myself in for.

CHAPTER TWO

"I thought you were going to destroy it?" I blinked bleary-eyed at the envelope Charity waggled at me as I entered the kitchen with a tray laden with dirty dishes. It was 6.30 a.m. and many of the production team were already at breakfast even though the sun was only just beginning to rise. Everybody was eager to get busy because this was the final day to get everything ready.

Today, the contestants were arriving, and I would be receiving endless deliveries of flour, caster sugar, eggs, chocolate, icing sugar, cherries, fondant, marzipan, food dyes, fresh and frozen fruit, vats of cream, spices, teas and the goddess only knew what else. Monsieur Emietter and my Ghostly Clean-Up Crew had emptied and deep-cleaned the inn's stores in order to make way for all the ingredients the contestants would need, but space would still be tight.

Here in the kitchen, ghosts bustled around me. Some were clearing up, others—under Monsieur Emietter's ghostly but beady eye—fried bacon and sausages, boiled or poached eggs, toasted bread and chopped tomatoes, cheese, ham and fruit. Juice was poured, tea and coffee brewed and decanted into smaller pots, and sauce boats refilled. I dodged around cutlery and bowls that flew through the air and deposited my tray of plates close to the sink where Ned was 'washing' dishes. No dishpan hands for Ned —he did it all by using his kinetic energy. None of the ghosts could interact with my physical plane, so they moved everything by utilising the power of thought. It was a sight I never tired of witnessing.

I returned to the kitchen door, heading for the bar area once more where the guests were breakfasting. From The Snug came the sound of about a million pages being printed. I'd set up an office in there for the producers and director after all, and they were organising schedules and menus and everything else they required.

All I needed to do was ready the remaining bedrooms, finalise lunch and dinner menus with

Monsieur Emietter, restock the bar and ensure all of our guests were happy and comfortable. Not much to ask in the grand scheme of things.

So why was Charity waving that rotten envelope at me?

"I *did* destroy it. I shredded it as you asked, and then I burned it in the grate in the bar. This is a new one."

Why had Sabien written two letters in such quick succession? He had to be desperate.

"Do the same to that one," I instructed, and Charity nodded.

A loud rapping on the back door hailed the arrival of the first delivery. I opened the door expecting a batch of groceries, and instead found myself signing for three enormous boxes filled with black and orange bunting.

"Cute," I said, inspecting the wares as the delivery driver disappeared. "What am I supposed to do with this lot? We don't want them in the kitchen or the rear stores."

Charity looked over my shoulder. "I'll call Zephaniah and we'll get them moved, shall we?"

"Good idea. I could ask Janice where she'd like it."

"Have you seen her this morning?" Charity asked. "Only she hasn't been down to breakfast yet."

"Maybe she's overslept." I lifted one of the boxes to line it up against the wall. They weren't particularly heavy. "I'll run upstairs and check on her, and ask whether she wants any breakfast. Would you mind stacking this lot?"

"No problem," Charity replied and came over to take a box, clamping the envelope between her teeth.

"Get rid of that letter first!" I growled.

A quick check of Janice's room on the second floor yielded no clue as to her whereabouts. Her bed *had* been slept in however, so I figured she might have used a different staircase to reach the bar area. I slipped back down to check but she still hadn't shown up for breakfast.

That meant she was either in someone else's room or she'd gone for a walk. I wasn't overly concerned. The sun had now breached the horizon and it looked set to be a decent day. The sky was clear and the clouds friendly and fluffy. A lovely morning for a stroll.

The dining area was noisy this morning—lots of

crew members with plenty to say to each other, buzzing in the build-up to the arrival of the contestants. Evidently the filming of the new series was an exciting venture. I overheard much enthusiastic speculation about the personalities and skills of the incoming contenders for the *Cake Off* crown. I couldn't help but thrill a little myself at the thought of observing the filming, but in the meantime I needed to turn my attention to clearing more plates from cluttered tables.

The crew sure had healthy appetites.

Above the general hubbub I thought I heard a high-pitched scream from outside, long and shrill. I paused in place, listening for it to come again, but there was nothing. I might have imagined it, but the sudden skipping of my heart, the sinking of my stomach and a little pulse beating behind my eye told me something different.

My witch twitch had been triggered.

It's one of the ghosts, I told myself. *Florence reliving her last moments as she sometimes does. Or maybe a member of the crew has dropped a stage weight on their toes. Or it'll be Janice having a meltdown because we haven't ordered enough of the right kind of flour.*

Trying not to draw attention to myself, I abandoned my pile of greasy plates on the nearest empty table and headed, as casually as possible, to the front door of the inn. I opened it and stood on the top step, gazing out at the lawn and the now fully erect marquee. I breathed in the fresh air, the scent of freshly cut grass, jasmine and gardenias. A glorious morning but the air was still and silent. Something—that scream, of course—had interrupted the dawn chorus.

By instinct more than anything else, I walked out onto the lawn and towards the marquee, walking around the expansive curve of canvas to get to the main entrance. As I rounded the final curve, I heard sobbing and scurried forwards in alarm.

A woman with a suitcase on wheels, wearing a long beige mackintosh and a tall traditional witch's hat, stood four or five feet away from the marquee's door flaps. Her hands were curled into fists, and she hiccoughed and sobbed into her thumbs, her shoulders heaving.

"Are you alright?" I cried and reached for her.

She shot backwards in alarm, tripping on her suitcase, and screamed again.

"It's okay. I'm the owner of the inn." I held my hands palm up, trying to pacify her.

She indicated inside the tent. I glanced over to

see what she had pointed at and spotted a pair of feet. Neat Mary Jane shoes, black patent leather with shiny buckles. Toes-up on the temporary flooring inside the marquee.

Janice? My first panicky thought. She'd collapsed —a lack of breakfast maybe. I always felt lightheaded if I skipped breakfast. Yes. That would be it. And I could fix that. I could help Janice.

Abandoning the newcomer to her sobs, I dashed inside the tent, but I skidded rapidly to a stop when I fully comprehended what I was seeing.

The woman's eyes stared sightlessly at the taut canvas of the marquee's ceiling, her arms lightly spread to each side of her.

She might have been resting, apart from the large silver cake knife embedded in her chest.

Somebody had murdered Janice Tork-Mimosa.

CHAPTER THREE

"Y̲ou're getting yourself quite the reputation."
DS George Gilchrist levelled an amused look
at me over the top of his notebook. I tried to decipher
whether the fluttering sensation in the pit of my
stomach was a reaction to finding the murdered
woman, or the fact that the handsome detective was
asking me questions.

He was right of course. We'd been in this position too many times now. George asking questions
and scribbling down my responses, and me trying to
explain how yet again I was at the centre of another
deadly mystery.

"It's not my personal choice," I responded tartly.
We had history, George and I, and it was too soon for
me to coat my words in honey. I noted the momentary look of hurt in his eyes and experienced a sharp

pang of regret. *If we could turn back the clock... we might have made it work.*

No. I'd had enough time travel to last me a lifetime.

"No, of course it isn't." His tone became tone brusque and professional. "So, anyway. Can you tell me how you knew Janice"—he checked his notebook —"Tork-Mimosa?"

I cast a glance towards the marquee. Scene of crime officers in white suits and bootees were coming and going. A flash of camera bulbs lit the canvas walls. "Well, I hadn't known her very long."

"Just a few days?"

I nodded. "In person, that is. I first met her a few days ago, but prior to that I'd exchanged a few emails with her."

"About?" George queried.

"About organising the delivery of goods for the production, hospitality arrangements, access to the site, that kind of thing."

"Could I have copies of those?" George asked.

I shrugged. "Of course. Anything you need. I'll print them out for you in a little while." *When you've finished interrogating me.*

"How did you find her?" George chewed on the end of his pen. "What was she like?"

I pondered on this for a second. Obviously I hadn't known her well. "It's difficult to say. My gut instinct is that she was really very nice."

"I'll take your gut instinct over many people's any day," George said, and I smiled at the compliment.

"Accommodating, organised, kind." I warmed to my subject, trying to analyse a person I'd barely spoken to. "Not someone who enjoyed conflict."

"Oh?" George raised his eyebrows. "Conflict? Why do you say that?"

"Well just that a couple of days ago, she was trying to calm down a situation with Patty Cake, the other producer, and—"

I stopped as George leaned in. He asked in a whisper, "Is that her *real* name? Patty Cake?"

"Yes." I shrugged.

"Genuinely? And she works on a baking programme?" A look of comic incredulity passed over George's face.

"I hadn't really thought about it," I said.

"It's daft, that's all."

"Lots of witches have what *you'd* consider to be daft names," I pointed out.

George frowned. "Patty Cake is a witch?"

"Of course she's a witch." Sometimes George

didn't quite get it. "Does *The Great Witchy Cake Off* not ring any bells with you? Everybody involved in the production is a witch. It's the highest rated cooking programme on Witchflix."

"Witchflix?"

I rolled my eyes. "George? Seriously?"

"I've never heard of it," George protested. "When do I have time to watch television?"

He had a point I supposed. He always seemed to be at work. "Ask Stacey then," I retorted. "I bet she's watched it."

George sighed and looked back down at his notebook. "Tell me about this situation from the other day."

"Patty decided she wanted to go and stay at The Hay Loft rather than here at Whittle Inn," I grumbled. "Janice was trying to smooth the waters. Raoul drove Patty over there."

"And he came back here afterwards?"

That made me think. "I don't know to be honest. I suppose so. I didn't see him at breakfast yesterday or today." I looked over at a crowd of people gathered on the steps. He wasn't among them. But in the distance I could make out his silver Tesla. "That's his car." I pointed it out to George. "So, he must be around. I don't think they're an item, but I couldn't swear to it." I lowered my voice to a whisper. "I think she's quite a bit older than she looks or would admit to."

George nodded and made a note of that. "Did anyone else have any beef with Janice?"

"Well I'm not sure Rob Parker was overly happy about her attitude to his sausage van when he showed up, but I really don't think you can pin this one on him." I indicated the Porky Perfection van tucked close to the front hedge. George positively drooled at the sight.

"Mmm. Parker's Porky Perfection. My favourite."

"You're so provincial." I tutted at him, but secretly I liked that he adored sausage, mash and gravy as much as I did.

The woman who had discovered the body was led past us by a female police officer. Her witch's hat was lopsided, and she dragged her case behind her, the wheels bumping along on the grass. "Who's that?" I asked.

George watched her being led to a police car. "Delores Everyoung. One of the contestants, apparently."

"Ah, of course." That made sense. "They're all due here today. She arrived early though. Why did she head straight for the marquee rather than check in at reception?" I hadn't heard a taxi come up the drive, but then given the noise levels at breakfast, perhaps one had come and gone and I was none the wiser.

"I don't know, Sherlock. But don't worry, I'm sure I can find out."

I kept my giggle in check. "Sorry, DS Gilchrist. I wasn't trying to do your job for you."

"Yeah? That would make a change," George said, and we laughed together, momentarily forgetting our differences and the solemn situation we found ourselves in.

A few hours later I carried a mug of strong coffee out of the inn and searched for George. I found him on his phone next to the police cordon. He finished his call and pocketed his phone. "We're almost done here," he told me. "I know the TV people are keen to get inside to finish setting up."

"You've been talking to them?" I asked.

"They've been talking at me," George groaned. "My goodness, that Patty Cake can go on." He glowered at me. "But yes. I don't think there's anybody within a mile radius that I haven't had words with today." He took the coffee from me gratefully and rubbed his eyes with his free hand. He looked tired. "Would you mind if I called a meeting in the bar later this afternoon? I'd like to fill everyone in on where we're at with the investigation."

"No problem," I said. "I'll sort out some refreshments for everyone too." I looked around for Florence. This would give her a chance to impress our guests. When I couldn't immediately spot her, I turned my attention back to George. "Any leads?"

"Nah. Nothing yet." He took a big gulp of coffee and moaned in happiness.

I tried another tack. "Cause of death was a large knife in the chest, I take it?"

George smirked. "We'll make a detective of you yet, Alf." He glanced around to make sure no-one was listening in, and leaned in. "Cause of death is likely to have been exsanguination. That's blood loss to you. Caused by a single stab wound through the heart." He paused, his brow wrinkling. "It was a vicious blow. Done in anger."

I grimaced.

"There was also a mark on her neck that we'll need a closer look at," George continued.

"Attempted strangulation?"

George shook his head. "No. It's more like a little burn."

"Do you have anybody in the frame?" I asked, pretending I knew what I was talking about and hadn't just watched too many Hollywood movies.

"No suspects at this time." We were standing so close together I could smell his aftershave. Such a familiar scent. I inhaled. He straightened up.

"So, erm, no suspects?" I repeated to cover my sudden confusion. "What about the woman who found her? Delores?"

"Seems unlikely. She doesn't appear to have any blood on her clothing. And whoever stabbed Janice will likely have some spatter on them. We've taken her to Exeter Police Station, and we'll have her clothing forensically analysed, of course, but I don't think we'll find anything." He looked me up and down. "You were next on the scene. Were you wearing those robes?"

I looked at what I had on. Dark charcoal robes. My best and newest set because I'd been hoping to impress Raoul a little, truth be told. "Yes."

"Maybe I should ask you to take those off." He uttered this double entendre without the slightest hint of humour. I cocked my head in astonishment, unable to immediately decipher his meaning. Was he *flirting* with me?

What about Stacey? I was about to ask, when a small figure ambled around the corner, drawing deeply on a cigarette.

The presenter, Mindi Blockweg.

For some reason I'd imagined that celebrities went around with perfect make-up and pristine clothing all the time, but Mindi appeared to be the exception to the rule. Dressed in a sloppy navy-blue jumper, a pair of linen cotton trousers that had seen better days and bright pink Crocs teamed with patterned socks, she had her short greasy hair tied up in tiny tight bunches and was puffing away like a steam train.

"Good afternoon, Officer. Alf," she said when she spotted us and exhaled a cloud of smoke. I took a couple of steps back, trying hard not to be impolite and wave the cloud of noxious air away. She squinted up at George. On television you couldn't tell how short she was, but she must barely have made five feet. "We spoke earlier, didn't we? I'm sorry I don't have my spectacles with me."

George smiled. "We did, Ms Blockweg. You haven't remembered anything new?"

"No. No, I haven't. It's a rum state of affairs the

more you think about it, isn't it? Janice was such a pleasant woman. If you were going to knock anyone off, surely you'd choose Patty."

"Why do you say that?" George asked, and scribbled something on his notepad.

Mindi shrugged. "It's no secret that Patty Cake is the driving force behind *The Great Witchy Cake Off*, but the programme was originally conceived by Janice. Patty made it happen, but Janice was the intellect behind it. Patty is a creative genius, but she's also... shall we say... challenging to work with. She takes no prisoners. She gets things done but she has a tendency to make enemies. Janice is—was—entirely more moderate in her approach. She liked to smooth things over. Keep people onside."

"So, do you think perhaps she hadn't managed to keep someone onside?" George asked with interest.

"If that's the case, I don't know who it might have been." Mindi twisted her face mournfully. "She often calmed situations, I know that much. The production meetings I was invited to back at HQ could be fraught at times."

"It sounds like Patty is quite a volatile character," I said. From what little I'd seen of her, there was no 'quite' about it. The woman was a grade A pain-in-the-proverbial. "Why do people put up with her attitude."

Mindi took a deep drag on her cigarette. "Have you seen the ratings for the programme? It's Witchflix's top rated cooking show. I mean, that's not to be treated lightly. It's a goldmine. Everyone involved in the show is well paid, and ultimately the guys running Witchflix understand—you don't bite the hand that feeds you. In our case, that hand ultimately belongs to Patty Cake. She's the *Witchy Cake Off* queen."

Exhaling one final time, Mindi dropped her cigarette into the grass and ground it out with the toe of her luminous shoe. "Witchflix royalty, in fact."

George pursed his lips, considering what Mindi had told us. "Any idea why Janice would have been in the marquee at that time of the morning? Was she looking for someone or something, do you know?"

Mindi reached into her trouser pocket and fished out a roll of mints. "I don't know, sorry. It's not unusual for the producers to check on the tent in the morning. As I said, Patty is the creative genius and she likes the tent to look just right for filming. I know the crew had finished installing the ovens and sinks yesterday and had been in there dressing the set with bunting and adding props till late last night. Maybe because she wasn't here, Janice decided she'd check up on everything instead. They both tend to start their day early."

Except now Janice would never again start another day. That knowledge hung over us all, and Mindi's shoulders sagged momentarily before she perked herself up and offered us each a mint. George took one. I declined. Call me fussy, but I couldn't be sure how long Mindi had stored those mints in her crumpled trousers.

"Thanks for the information." George popped his sweet in his mouth.

"Any time." Mindi nodded and strolled away.

We watched her go. "It's peculiar, isn't it?" I asked George. "Nobody has a bad word to say about Janice and yet everyone talks about Patty being difficult. It's like Snow White versus the evil queen."

George snorted. "An old folks' version of it at least. Janice was hardly the lovely Snow White character, was she?"

"That's a bit ageist of you, George," I said. I motioned in Mindi's direction. "She seems like an intelligent woman, and yet she has no awareness of any negative character traits Janice might have had? I find that hard to believe. Surely you don't become successful in the film and television business without having a spine of steel? I heard how she spoke to Rob Parker the other day. She was pretty sharp with him, and if that's the case there will have been others. Janice must have annoyed plenty of people at one time or another."

"People don't like to speak ill of the dead, Alf. You have to remember that in my line of work."

I grunted. "Well how do you ever get at the truth then?"

"You go back to them. Several times if necessary. Give them a poke. The more water that flows under the bridge, the looser the tongue becomes."

That made sense. "So you'll just give people time to remember Janice properly then?"

"I will." George smiled and tapped my arm. "As I said, we'll make a detective of you yet, Alf."

CHAPTER FOUR

ater that afternoon almost the entire production crew, the presenters and the contestants assembled in the bar to discuss the situation with George and his team. The whole inn had been temporarily given over to the needs of the production, so I didn't have to worry about accommodating any other guests. George took his place at the bar itself in order to command everyone's attention from the front.

A new producer had turned up to take Janice's place. This seemed slightly hasty to me, but I suppose television is one of those cut-throat worlds, and the Witchflix bosses couldn't afford too long a delay before they resumed filming.

Her name was Murgatroyde Snippe, and she cut a compelling figure. I reckoned she was my about age, perhaps slightly older. Of average height, with short dark hair, she favoured men's tailoring and was therefore wearing a shirt and thin paisley tie under a dark grey suit, teamed with black leather Classic Oxford shoes. This jarred slightly with the amount of make-up she was wearing. I'd never seen foundation applied quite as thickly before. You could have scraped it off with a trowel.

Florence quietly zipped around between tables, depositing plates of goodies—finger-size cakes and pastries—for the assembled throng to tuck into, and while there were some red eyes and a lack of appetite in some quarters, many others present tucked in with gusto. Once or twice I overheard exclamations of delight and spotted Florence flitting to the table in question, carefully inspecting what they were eating, before dashing back to the bar where I observed her scribbling something down with a pencil on a piece of paper.

"Florence," I hissed. "Florence! What are you doing?"

She floated towards me, her eyebrows raised in genuine seriousness. "I'm making a note of the cakes everyone likes, Miss Alf. It's research."

"Research?"

"Yes, you know. Into the flavours and textures

people prefer. It will be useful information when I'm baking for our guests in the future."

"I see," I said. "But to be honest, Florence, all of your cakes are so good I doubt anyone will be complaining."

"But we have baking royalty here at the inn, Miss Alf. I want to make sure I do my very best."

Florence swirled about to gape at Faery Kerry with wide fangirl eyes. The faery sat alongside Boo Sully and Murgatroyde Snippe at a large round table. The rest of the production crew huddled together at the other side of the room. I wondered if there was some sort of unspoken hierarchy. Maybe some rivalry. No doubt George would have noticed, but I decided I'd mention it to him anyway.

I understood Florence wanting to do her best. I leaned towards her and whispered, "Has Faery Kerry tried any of your sugary treats yet?"

Florence shook her head, hardly able to tear her gaze away. "Not yet. I really wish she would, Miss Alf. I'm trying to keep an eye on her. I don't want to miss her reaction, but I'm not actually sure she eats anything."

Faery Kerry—the most famous of the judges— had been a celebrity cook for decades prior to the commissioning of the show. She'd written dozens of books on baking, including one bestseller entirely devoted to the art of creating faery cakes. I knew Florence had devoured this title from cover to cover on many occasions.

"I'm sure she will soon." I tried to be reassuring. "I'll keep an eye out too."

"Thank you, Miss Alf."

"Mmm. This macaron is delicious. What's the flavour, do you think?" a technician sitting close to the front of the room was enquiring of her neighbour.

Florence sped to the woman's side. "It's passion fruit, Miss," she enthused, and began to run through the other flavours on offer.

George called the meeting to order. "Good afternoon everyone. Thank you all for making yourself available—"

"Not everyone is here yet," a voice interrupted him from the main doorway. Mindi stood half in and half out of the room. I couldn't see it, but I imagined she had a cigarette on the go and was trying to keep it quiet. I frowned. There was absolutely no smoking allowed on the premises.

I glanced around the bar area. Neither Patty Cake nor Raoul were in attendance. Come to think of it, I hadn't seen Patty all day.

"Who's missing?" George asked.

"Raoul went to pick Patty up from wherever it is she's staying," Mindi told us helpfully, then disappeared back outside to finish off her cigarette. "Here they are," her discombobulated voice called through a few seconds later.

Wearing a knee-length black dress, shiny black stilettos, with a black silk scarf tied artfully around her hair and a pair of sunglasses that—if anything— were darker than the ones she'd been sporting over the previous few days, Patty drifted slowly into the room casting a melancholy glance around at everyone gathered before her.

"I'm so sorry to keep you waiting, my darlings," she offered in a husky voice. "Only—" She raised a crisp white handkerchief and dabbed at her eyes. Raoul, who had followed her in, took her by the elbow and led her to a seat next to Faery Kerry.

Patty nodded at Murgatroyde. "They've sent you, have they?"

"The office thought you'd appreciate the support," Murgatroyde replied.

Patty dabbed at her cheeks. "They didn't waste much time. Poor Janice."

Murgatroyde set her jaw. "Indeed. It's a terrible thing."

"Can I get you some tea or coffee?" Charity

approached Patty's table and interrupted, her voice low and respectful. Murgatroyde seemed relieved at the disruption. Florence bustled over and set down some cups and saucers and a tray of nibbles.

"Coffee. Black," Patty requested and Charity scuttled back to the bar.

I remained in my position next to the fireplace observing Patty with some curiosity. Was this demonstration of emotion only for effect or did she genuinely lament the loss of her co-producer?

Unless the murderer had followed Janice to Whittlecombe, or Janice's death had been completely random, it seemed more than likely that the killer was hiding in plain sight in this very room.

I shivered at the thought. We always kept a fire going in the bar during the day, no matter what the weather. This was a large room to heat, and the stone walls meant it was cool even during the height of the summer. And besides, you can't beat a proper fire to create atmosphere, can you? Today though, I couldn't help thinking of the cosy environment as a rotten apple. Something putrid lay at the heart of Whittle Inn.

It wasn't welcome.

Casting one final glance at Patty, who swivelled her head to look at me, I directed my attention to

George. At the front of the room, he cleared his throat and consulted his notes once more.

"Okay, I think we can begin now." He looked up to check on Mindi, who had returned to the room and closed the front door behind her.

"As I was saying. Thank you all for attending this meeting. I thought it was important to run a few things by you while you're all in situ." He looked pointedly at Patty. "Now, it goes without saying that you should each have spoken to a member of my team, and if you haven't already done so, I would respectfully ask you to remain behind after the meeting to remedy that." There was a small murmur of consent.

"On behalf of my team, I would like to offer my condolences on the loss of Janice Tork-Mimosa. I know from speaking with many of you that she was well loved and will be sorely missed. I can categorically assure you that we will do our utmost to catch the person who did this, but of course we will require your assistance."

George glanced around the room. "It would greatly assist my investigation if your whereabouts are known at all times, and I would ask you not to leave the inn or the grounds until a member of my team gives the go-ahead."

"Preposterous," a sharp voice piped up.

Everyone in the room swivelled their heads from George to the source of the interruption.

Patty. Who else?

"I'm not even residing here. Of course I need to leave the grounds."

Raoul smiled at George. "Patty is staying at the other inn in the village."

"Oh, I see. I wasn't aware." George had a quick word with one of his colleagues who must have confirmed this. "Then I would ask that you don't leave the village, Ms Cake."

Patty, still wearing her sunglasses, fixed him in her sights. "Entirely unnecessary," she spat. "I can assure you I had absolutely nothing to do with this."

"That's as maybe—" George began.

"If you didn't do the crime, you won't do the time," Faery Kerry offered, and her soft musical laughter tinkled around the room.

I studied the elderly faery with renewed interest. She seemed to be taking the death of Janice fairly well.

"Ridiculous," Patty muttered, but she settled back in her chair and held her tongue. Faery Kerry might have been the only person in the room who could nay-say Patty.

"Do you have any inkling who was responsible, Detective?" Mindi asked from the rear of the room, and George's face brightened as he turned away from the disgruntled Patty.

"Not at this time, but we're looking into a number of leads," he responded with a confidence that that almost had me convinced.

"I assume you don't think anybody else is in danger?" Raoul asked, and George flashed his calm, confident smile once more.

"We're working on the premise that this was a one-off. Someone who had a grudge against Janice."

"Does that mean we can all go back to work?" Murgatroyde asked. I was surprised when George nodded.

"We're clearing the scene as quickly as possible. So, I think yes. You'll be able to resume shortly. Within an hour or so."

"I'm not sure I want to," moaned a young woman with coloured paint all over her hands. One of the set dressers I surmised. There were mutters of agreement.

"I can understand that, and it is of course entirely up to each individual, but as I've stated, we do think this is a one-off and we would ask you to remain within the grounds for the next few days, or at least not to leave the village." George shot Patty a sharp look. "Now, does anyone have any more questions?"

"Of course, it doesn't have to be one of us that's the culprit at all, does it?" Raoul Scurrysnood's growl rolled around the room and everyone turned to look at him.

"What do you mean?" George asked politely.

Raoul's twinkling green eyes sought me out. "Just that it may not have been somebody from the production who killed Janice. It might have been someone from the inn."

The accusation hit me in the chest, and I struggled to retain my composure. Blood pumped loudly in my ears. Time and time again Whittle Inn and its inhabitants were the subject of accusation and conjecture. I couldn't help but take it personally.

I opened my mouth to offer a sharp retort when Mindi suddenly piped up, "The person who found her? Who was that?"

George studied his notebook. "That was Delores Everyoung. She has been escorted to the police station for questioning, but she'll be back a little later."

"One of the contestants." Boo Sully flicked through the notes on his clipboard. "Oh my. I do hope she'll be alright. We start filming the day after tomorrow."

"She was a little shocked, but we'll get her sorted and deliver her back here as soon as possible," one of George's team promised.

"She's not a suspect then?" Mindi again.

George used his stern voice. "*Everyone* is a suspect at this stage. The crew, the production team, the contestants... and yes, even the permanent inhabitants of Whittle Inn and surrounds."

I shuffled in my spot next to the fire and glared at George. He deliberately avoided my gaze.

"How exciting!" Boo clasped a hand to his heart. "I've always wanted to be involved in a real-life police investigation."

I opened my mouth in astonishment. Were these people for real? Had they failed to understand that their friend—or at least colleague—was gone forever? She wouldn't be coming back. Some of the people here behaved as though this murder was all part of the show.

Something that would boost the ratings.

I frowned.

Boost the ratings? Was that me being cynical?

Or was that *really* what was at the heart of all this?

CHAPTER FIVE

"You ought to keep your own hens at the inn." Millicent Ballicott gazed down at the double-tiered tray of eggs I balanced in my grasp as her dogs, Jasper the lurcher and Sunny the Yorkie, sniffed around my feet.

I grimaced. "It has crossed my mind. But I'm not sure I'd be very good with chickens."

Millicent clucked for effect. A plump and good-natured lady of advancing years, she was my closest witchy neighbour outside any who temporarily inhabited the inn. Known for her eccentric dress sense—today she was sporting forest-green tights with a lemon-yellow sundress, a gruesome brown handknitted cardigan and a straw hat decorated with plastic sunflowers—she'd proven herself as a good friend to me time and time again.

"Why would you worry? You don't have to look

after them," Millicent laughed. "Just find a ghost to do the job for you. You have an inn full of them and many of them could do with some worthwhile employment."

She was right. I had an attic full of ghosts who hardly lifted a translucent finger on a daily basis. I called on them when I needed them, but now that the inn had been fully renovated and I had ghosts attending to cleaning and maintenance, the rest of them were hardly ever called upon.

"Chickens aren't scared of ghosts then?" I asked doubtfully.

Millicent shrugged. "I don't see why they would be. They have no reason to be, do they?"

She had a point, I supposed. My mother Yasmin had kept chickens in a little hen coop, at the shack where she'd lived out the end of her life. I had never been overly fond of them, but it was true—I spent an absolute fortune on eggs from Whittle Stores.

"Maybe I'll look into it," I said, wondering what my little familiar, Mr Hoo, would have to say if I introduced more birds to the inn.

"I think—" Millicent's words were drowned out by the throbbing snarl of a deep-throated engine whizzing past us—far too quickly for the slow speed limit—and I turned in surprise as a classic MG in

British racing green, music blaring above the roar, screeched as it turned into the drive leading to The Hay Loft's car park.

"One of your current guests?" Millicent asked in amusement.

"I don't believe so." I hadn't recognised the male driver and as far as I knew, only Patty Cake was staying at The Hay Loft. Everyone else was either with me or camping in trailers behind Whittle Inn. I placed my hand on my heart. "Ooh, he made me jump with that racket."

"You're getting old, Alf," Millicent laughed.

"I am. I prefer the quiet life."

The tinkle of a bicycle bell alerted us to Sally McNab-Martin's arrival. She jumped gracefully off her bike and greeted us and the dogs. "Good morning, ladies!"

"How are you, Sally?" I asked. "Everything alright with the cottage?"

Sally's abusive relationship with her soon-to-be-ex-husband had come to light while I'd been plying my trade as a fortune teller at the Psychic Fayre a few months ago. Once I'd returned to my normal life at Whittle Inn, I'd offered her the tenancy for Primrose Cottage. It had been standing empty since the death of poor Derek Pearce, and it seemed fitting that it should go to someone who was already a popular member of Whittlecombe's community. Sally, like Millicent, was active in the WI and raised money for several local charities.

"Everything is just fine and dandy, Alf," she smiled. "Thank you. A glorious day for a bike ride, isn't it? The trees are just beginning to change colour. You can smell autumn on its way."

As we all remarked on the glorious weather, the little green MG suddenly spun back out of The Hay Loft's car park and across the road, pulling up in front of us.

A slightly overweight chap, early forties perhaps, with a full head of fair hair, mirrored sunglasses and a deep tan hailed us. "Ladies!"

We turned around as one and stared into the MG. He pulled the handbrake on and pushed his sunglasses away from his face onto the top of his head.

"So sorry to interrupt your gossiping." My hackles instantly rose. "I was wondering whether there was anywhere around here with a decent off-licence?"

"Whittle Stores?" Millicent indicated the little shop behind us.

"No, no, no. That won't do." The man dismissed

her suggestion with an offhand wave of his fingers. "I'm looking to buy some high-end wine, maybe a little champagne."

"Whittle Stores sells champagne," I told him, lifting my chin in defence of the perceived slur on my friends Rhona and Stan. The man in the car reminded me of somebody. Not in a good way.

"There's a large supermarket in Honiton," Sally offered. "It has a really good selection of wines and spirits."

The man harrumphed. "That sounds like just the ticket! The spirits aren't an issue. Lyle's got plenty of those." He nodded his head at The Hay Loft, owned by my arch-rival Lyle Cavendish. "But yes, some decent wine would go down a storm. So which way is Honiton?" He addressed this to Sally, who slipped her bicycle onto its side stand and leaned into the car in an effort to give the driver directions.

Her instructions only seemed to confuse him, although I was fairly sure that if he followed the road signs he'd eventually get where he needed to be. This was East Devon after all. You either drove inland or you ended up in the sea. There weren't many other options.

"How about you take me with you?" Sally said,

after he'd frowned and asked her to repeat them more than once. "It will be much easier, and I have the time."

"Sally," I gasped, holding out a restraining arm. We didn't know the man from Adam. He might have been anyone.

"Oh, it's quite alright." The man in the car winked at me. "I'm Crispin Cavendish. Lyle is my big brother. I'm staying with him for a few days, hoping to lure him to do a little business with me. You can trust me, I assure you."

"There you are!" Sally said triumphantly. "He's practically a local!" Without further ado she jumped into the passenger seat of the MG, abandoning her bicycle where it stood. "I'm Sally McNab-Martin," she told him. "Pleased to meet you."

"Likewise." He shook her hand and then released the handbrake. The MG sprang away with an ear-splitting squeal, leaving both Millicent and me spitting out dust in its wake, astonished by the turn of events.

"Can you believe that?" I had to blink rapidly to try and clear grit from my eyes. I still had a tight hold of four dozen eggs and no free hands.

Millicent shook her head and sighed. "Young women today! That woman has no sense. Out of the frying pan and into the fire. She finally gets rid of one awful man, but then has her head turned by the next fellow who comes along driving a flash motor."

"What is the world coming to?" I tutted, like the old dear I hoped I wasn't going to turn into for at least another forty years.

Millicent tittered. "I guess, unlike the pair of us, she still has some 'pulling' power."

I sniffed. "I have pulling power," I protested weakly. "If I want it..."

That only made Millicent laugh harder. I pouted.

"Well," I sniffed, "I have to get back to the inn. *George* will be there." I emphasised my ex-beau's name.

"What are we going to do with Sally's bicycle?" Millicent asked. I had my hands full and she had a bag of shopping and the dogs to juggle.

"Maybe Rhona will keep an eye on it?" I suggested. "We could wheel it closer to the shop."

"Do you need some help?" A polite voice interrupted us. I turned to see a tall, geeky-looking man of around my age, wearing a flowered shirt with maroon trousers and round spectacles. Another stranger to the village. Whittlecombe was being overrun with them.

"Alex! Hello!" Millicent cried. "When did you get home?"

"Only this morning, Mrs Ballicott. How lovely to see you again."

Millicent gave the young man a one-armed hug, and he kissed her cheek. I looked on with interest.

"Alf—" Millicent made the introductions. "This is Alex Bramble. Mr Bramble's youngest son. I don't know whether you've met before. Alex is a lecturer in York."

"Oh, how lovely," I said as Alex reached out to shake my hand. I held my trays of eggs up in the air until he got the message that I couldn't reciprocate. He flushed in embarrassment and dropped his head. "Nice to meet you," I said, trying to ease his discomfort.

"Alex, this is Alfhild Daemonne. She's the owner of Whittle Inn."

"Pleased to meet you." Alex pulled a face at Millicent. "Although unfortunately, I'm between jobs at the moment, Mrs Ballicott. My college was restructured, and they had to let me go so I'm looking for work."

"Oh, that *is* a shame," said Millicent, and I nodded along with her. "I'm sure you'll find something. Maybe closer to home."

"That would be nice. See the old folk a little more often."

"Exactly," Millicent concurred. "Perhaps you can find something to tide you over in the meantime. Alf was just saying she needs someone to look after chickens."

I stared at Millicent in surprise. "I'm not sure I said that at all, Millicent."

"It's something to think about though. Isn't it, my dear?" Millicent grinned at me saucily. I shook my head at the matchmaking cheek of my friend.

My arms were aching by the time I began making my way up the long drive leading to the inn. As I rounded the trees that towered over the narrow strip of lane, I could see the marquee in all its glory. Decorated with an array of coloured bunting in purple, black and orange, it stood proud in front of my equally striking wonky inn.

My inn suffered from some sort of architectural anomaly, much like the leaning tower of Pisa. It leaned firstly in one direction and then overcompensated in the other on the second storey. There were turrets on every corner and a number of tall chimneys reaching for the skies above the thatched roof. Painted in black and white, as you'd expect for a Tudor inn, it had diamond glass in the windows. It dated back at least to the Elizabethan age, if not before. To my mind at least, it was a work of art.

Raoul's car, along with several others belonging to crew and contestants, was tucked at the side of the inn close to Jed's van, out of shot of the cameras. Several police cars and a forensic examination vehicle were parked on the drive between the marquee and the inn. As I rounded the final bend I heard a van behind me, so I stepped over to the verge as Rob Parker drove past, heading for his space on the edge of the garden.

George appeared as if by magick (not of my doing for once) and waved Rob down. I joined them in front of the inn as Rob clambered out of his cab.

"How're you doing, Detective?" Rob asked George.

"I'm fine thanks, Rob." George sniffed the air. The faint scent of sausages and rich gravy clung to the van. "I need to ask you a few questions if you don't mind?"

Rob pulled a face. A few months ago, George had saved Rob's life by pulling him from his burning food truck. Since then they'd been on good terms. I couldn't imagine that Rob had anything to hide.

"You want to talk about the murder?" Rob swallowed.

George brandished his pen and notebook. "Would that be okay? It won't take long."

"What do you need to know?"

"How much did you have to do with Janice Tork-Mimosa?"

Rob waggled his head. "I didn't know her name. I turned up here the day before yesterday. Alf here invited me. This Janice—if that's who she was—seemed a little rude, to be frank. I don't think she liked the idea of me serving sausages to the folk they have staying here."

George looked at me and I nodded. "Rob's here at my invitation. Under the terms of the contract with Witchflix, I have to provide a range of food and beverages. Cater for all tastes, you know? I thought Rob would be perfect for cosy, comforting meals."

George nodded his approval. "Good thinking." He turned back to Rob. "So that was the only time you spoke to Janice?"

Rob shuffled uneasily. "Mmm. Not exactly."

"That's a no? So you spoke to her again? When would that have been?"

Rob stroked his chin. "A few hours later. I'd set everything up, had the fryers going. A big pot of mash. Gravy. The works." George smiled and nodded. "I'd served a few members of the crew and word was getting around, but people were very busy setting up the marquee, so I knew it might be a late shift."

"And Janice came over to visit you?" George clarified. "What time was that? Roughly?"

"She did. Maybe eight-ish. It was already dark."

George scribbled the time down on a page already full of notes. "And what did she say to you?"

"She apologised for our earlier encounter. She was very pleasant actually. Apparently the other lady had been winding her up."

"Patty Cake?" I wondered aloud.

Rob shrugged. "I don't know. She didn't explain herself. Just sounded genuinely apologetic."

"Did you talk about anything else?" George asked.

"We had a discussion about the provenance of my sausages." A look of triumph crossed Rob's face. "If she was trying to catch me out, she failed. You know as well as anyone that I know precisely where my meat comes from. Down to the actual farm. I even use onions and potatoes that have been grown in Devon. The only thing that isn't local is the mushy peas, and that's only because the best mushy peas come from upcountry."

I couldn't help chipping in. "Did you convince her?"

"I think so, yes. I even persuaded her to take some away with her."

He did? "What did she have?" I asked, curious to find out.

Rob cast his mind back. "She had our sausages with sage and onion and some mash and gravy."

"Good choice," George approved.

"Mmm," I said, non-committedly. Rob regarded me with a frown. "I mean, mmm. Yum. Yes. Yummy," I said hurriedly. "Although I prefer my sausages in cider."

"Ha! They're my best sellers." Rob nodded, his smile returning now that he knew I wasn't casting aspersions on his famous sausages. "Is that it, then?" he asked George, who closed his notebook with a snap.

"Yes, that's all for now. Thanks for your time."

"You know where to find me if you need anything else," Rob said, pulling open the door of his van and climbing into the front seat. "Like dinner."

He started the engine and the van lurched off

along the drive and then onto the grass, heading for a space in the corner.

"Well, at any rate," said George. "If all that's true, it looks like Janice and Rob made up. I didn't think he could possibly be a suspect."

I shuffled in place. My arms, still propping up the tray of eggs, were aching. "I wouldn't be too sure of that."

"Why?" George offered up his own hands to take the eggs from me, but I shook my head.

"Because I happen to know that Janice ate in the bar that night. Monsieur Emietter had cooked baked cod with a spicy crust and served it with sea vegetables and chilli and cumin-infused puy lentils."

"What in Heaven's name are sea vegetables?" asked George in disgust. "Is this some sort of witchy fae thing? Do you have an 'undersea' gardener digging a plot in the silt and producing blue carrots and salty green turnips?"

"You're such a philistine, George." I smirked. "It's seaweed."

"Seaweed?" George gagged and I laughed out loud. "Ugh!"

"She had rhubarb panna cotta for dessert. Florence made that."

George shuddered. "Well, that sounds nicer."

Then it dawned on him what I was saying. "You're saying she ate two courses of food at what time?"

"That would have been around nine, I suppose. Or just after."

"So if we believe Rob, she polished off his sausage and mash and then headed into the inn to eat—ugh—sea vegetables, cod and rhubarb."

"Yes." I didn't want to disbelieve Rob, but facts were facts.

"She certainly had a healthy appetite." George looked thoughtfully at Rob's van in the distance. "Or Rob's lying."

CHAPTER SIX

L unch was being served in the dining area of
the bar when I finally deposited my eggs on
the counter in the kitchen. I ducked past flying pans
and knives as the ghosts working around me directed
their tools of the trade just above my head with
unerring accuracy. Everything happened at top
speed in here during service, and as a rule it paid to
stay out of the way, but I had to deliver them.

Florence was bending over one of the counters,
adding the final touches to some gaily coloured
French fancies. They were decorated in gaudy
orange and deep lilac icing, with teeny tiny cats on
black and orange iced tartan blankets. They must
have taken her hours to do.

"Oh no," she replied airily when I asked. "It's
only a vanilla sponge traybake cut into squares. The

secret is the crème filling." She offered me the bowl with the remains of something purple inside. I scooped a little out with my pinkie and delicately touched my finger to my tongue. An unmistakeable touch of lavender.

"Lovely!" I said and reached for one of the finished fancies.

"Miss Alf!" Florence chastised me. "Guests first."

I pulled a face but took her point.

"Florence—" I changed the subject. "Do you recall Janice eating dinner at the inn last night?"

"The lady who was murdered, Miss?" She nodded. "I do. Funny thing though."

"Why?" I asked.

"Well... I served her and she had the fish, but she didn't eat very much of it. Then when I cleaned her room on the morning of the murder, I found a discarded takeaway."

"Let me guess. Sausage and mash?"

"That's right."

Puzzled, I reached out absently to try and take one of Florence's cakes again, but she whisked them away from me. "Had she eaten much of it?" I asked.

Florence shrugged. "Well, I didn't look very

closely. But there was an awful lot there, so I imagine not. It had made the room very smelly. I had to air it out and spray my favourite air freshener."

"*L'attention! L'attention!*"

Monsieur Emietter was ready to send the soup. I peered inside the tureen as it moved past me: a beautifully scented bouillabaisse. Served with croutons and a lemon drizzle, it would be perfect for lunch. For those who preferred something a little... well... English, there were toasted cheese and tomato sandwiches, baby pork pies and a range of healthy-looking salads.

I snagged a toasted sandwich as the serving platter went by and bit into it. The cheese instantly burnt the roof of my mouth and I cried out. Monsieur Emietter directed a stern look my way. Suitably chastised, I dropped it and headed for the cloakroom to give my hands a good wash. Charity could no doubt use my help in the dining room.

We'd agreed with the producers—Janice specifically—that we wouldn't serve alcohol until each day's work had been successfully completed, and so although Zephaniah, my one-armed jack-of-all-trades, was operating the bar for soft drinks and so on, there was little need for me there. Instead I grabbed a tray and helped the guests to servings of potato salad. There was plenty to go around; nobody would ever starve at Whittle Inn, despite me having a French chef.

"Miss Alf?" Florence appeared at my elbow, looking slightly worried.

"Is everything alright, Florence?" I asked.

Florence nodded at Faery Kerry, sitting with Patty Cake, Raoul Scurrysnood and Boo Sully on a table by themselves. "Miss Alf, please don't serve them too much of the main course. I'd like to make sure they have room for a cake."

"Hasn't Faery Kerry tried one of your cakes yet, Florence?" I asked in surprise.

"Not that I'm aware, Miss."

"Leave it to me," I said. "I'm on the case."

I took a few steps towards the judges' table and could have sworn I heard Florence mutter, "That may not play out in my favour, Miss Alf." But when I turned to check, she only smiled at me.

"Is everything alright with your lunch?" I asked, beaming around at the four *Cake Off* bigwigs. I noted a space had been left for Mindi, but she was nowhere in sight. Probably outside having a crafty puff.

"Just perfect, thank you," Faery Kerry nodded graciously. She'd ordered the soup, but from the amount still in her bowl, it looked like she wasn't going to finish it. Similarly, Patty had the minutest serving of bouillabaisse and she hadn't even lifted her spoon to it.

"Is that potato salad?" Raoul sat up straighter, trying to peer into the silver serving bowl I was carrying.

"Yes," I said, lifting it higher and out of his eyeline. "I need to refresh it. We appear to be running out." Potato salad can be very filling after all, and I didn't want to ruin his appetite. "I'll be right back to offer you a refill." I had no intention of coming back, of course, and I hid around the corner until their plates were eventually cleared by an attentive Florence.

At that moment Charity began to bring out bowls of fruit salad and freshly whipped cream. I sidled up to her. "None for the judges' table," I hissed, and Charity gaped at me in surprise.

"But—"

I widened my eyes at her and then nodded in Florence's direction as the housekeeper whizzed past us to deliver plates of French fancies to every table. Charity frowned but swerved around the judges' table and made for the contestants instead.

Florence served her plates of pretty French

fancies to every table before finally plucking up the courage to approach Faery Kerry and Raoul. They paid her little attention, but Mindi chose that moment to walk into the bar and take her place.

"Oooh, aren't these cute!" she said in a loud voice, plucking one from the serving platter and twisting it this way and that to get a better look at the cat's tiny sculpted face. "Too nice to eat." With that, she took an enormous bite of the cake, chomping straight through the cat on the blanket. She chewed with relish. "Mmm. Mmm. Mmmmm. Ohmigosh," she said with her mouth still full. "So good." Florence, floating next to the table, smiled so wide that for a second, I could almost imagine her little round cheeks glowing with pleasure.

However, given that ghosts don't gain colour, she remained pale, merely luminescing a little brighter.

"Seriously," Mindi was telling Raoul and Faery Kerry. "I know I'm only a lowly presenter and you're the great gods of the judging world, but you should try these."

"Oh, I really can't eat another thing," Patty mumbled, although the evidence suggested she hadn't consumed anything.

"I wasn't talking to you," Mindi retorted. "Raoul, wrap your laughing gear around one of these." She picked up the platter and held it out to him.

Looking like he'd heard it all before, Raoul gave Mindi a one-sided smirk and picked up one of the delicate fancies. He placed it on the plate and, unlike Mindi, politely utilised his dessert fork to cut into the sponge. He lifted the fork and scrutinised the texture and colour of the cake, gave it a sniff and raised his eyebrows in agreeable surprise before taking a bite.

He nodded at Faery Kerry, who was altogether more delicate. She broke off a tiny amount and popped it onto the end of her tongue, then ran it around her mouth a little before trying a tiny bit more.

"Delicious!" she announced, and a number of the contestants looked around from their own table to see whom she was casting judgement on.

If Florence could have died and gone to heaven a second time, I think she would have done so. She half sank to the floor, then in jubilation, shot into the air before streaking around the outskirts of the bar and dining area. Round she went, once, twice, three times.

Faery Kerry beckoned me over. "Who made these delicious cakes? Someone in your kitchen?"

"Yes," I replied. "Florence. My housekeeper.

She's a wonderful baker. She'll be so pleased you enjoyed these."

"More than enjoyed. These are sensational!"

Sitting alongside the faery, Patty frowned and reached for one of the fancies. She didn't bother moving the cake to her plate, just dug her fingers into the icing, pinching off a chunk from the side. She popped it into her mouth and chewed. It was difficult to see her expression, hiding as she was behind her customary sunglasses, but for a fraction of a second she remained very still, and the sides of her lips curled up.

Patty glanced at Faery Kerry, who looked at Raoul. Nobody consulted Boo.

Raoul nodded. "You know... we're a contestant down. Delores Everyoung chose to back out of the competition. I think your Florence would make a great replacement."

"Well. Hmm. Let me see." I pretended a nonchalance I was far from feeling when actually you could have knocked me down with a feather. "I'll have to ask her, of course, and then find a replacement for her here at the inn for the duration of the filming of the show."

I turned about to see Florence hovering behind

Charity's shoulder, listening to every word that was said.

I clenched my fists and mouthed, "Oh my witchy goodness!" at my housekeeper, but I'm not sure she saw me do it. Florence, eternally pale anyway, had fainted dead away.

CHAPTER SEVEN

"So, we have yet another dead body at the inn, and the place is crawling with the police once more. I have numerous celebrity bakers in residence, and Florence is going to be famous," I explained to Mr Hoo. "That about sums up the past few days."

My feathered friend had chosen to perch on a low branch near to the bench I occupied in the clearing of Speckled Wood. It felt like it had been a rather full-on day, what with contracts to review, murder cases to investigate and strange men turning up in Whittlecombe. As I often did of an evening, I'd taken a little time for myself and walked into the heart of my wood.

"I hope it doesn't go to her head," I added. "What if she becomes so popular she's invited to write a baking column for *The Celestine Times*? Or maybe even write a cookbook? I've seen it happen.

Some previous *Cake Off* contestants have been able to travel the world, or they go on and make other television programmes." I could see it now. *Barbequing the Florence Way*. Or *A Thousand Smoky Recipes for Halloween*. She'd make the perfect cover girl.

"Hoo-ooo."

"I'd miss her. That's all." My voice sounded thin in the stillness of the wood.

"Hooooo."

"I know. But she's my friend, not just an employee. She never has been. Besides, I don't even pay her." I twiddled with a strand of my hair, preoccupied by the history Florence and I had shared during our time together at the inn. "She drives me crazy at times."

"Hoo-oo. Oooh ooh."

"What do you mean I drive *you* crazy at times? You can talk. Well, you can't talk—"

"Hoo-ooo!"

"Okay you *can* talk. But only in owl." I smiled at Mr Hoo. "I suppose we both drive each other a little nuts, huh?"

"Hoo. Hoo." Mr Hoo wiggled his head in agreement and proceeded to engage in a little dance on his branch. "Hooooo."

"I'm glad I have you too."

We lapsed into companionable silence. From deeper in the wood I could hear the sound of music —*Greensleeves*. A lute. The notes drifted prettily towards us on a light breeze.

"Must be Luppitt," I said. I often banished Luppitt Smeatharpe and his Elizabethan band of Devonshire Brothers into the wood when they wanted to rehearse. Luppitt was a ghost from the Elizabethan period that I'd kind of adopted, and I loved him to bits, but the blaring of the crumhorn and the crashing of the drums could get a bit too much for me and my guests at times, and sometimes the singing was just a little too melancholic.

However, given the lateness of the hour and the sweetness with which the lute found the notes for this magnificent English tune, supposedly written by Henry VIII, I was curious. "Shall we go and investigate?" I asked Mr Hoo, and he stopped dancing and regarded me with solemn eyes.

"Hooooooooo. Hooo oo."

"Why would I be intruding?" I asked, puzzled by Mr Hoo's comment.

These were my woods after all. Well—I liked to think of them as my woods, but it had been established, rather forcibly on the part of my great-grandmother, that actually, I was a mere custodian of the woods and the inn. My sole purpose of being here was to maintain the building and the grounds and keep them safe for past and present generations of Daemonnes and their friends and neighbours to enjoy.

I crept along the path, heading towards the music; Mr Hoo remained behind me, twittering with indignation from a safe distance. I found myself at the edge of the pool that Vance, an enormous oak tree and The Keeper of the Marsh, inhabited. I could see him there. He shimmied, waving his branches along to the music, as though conducting some kind of forest orchestra.

Luppitt stood with one foot elevated on a rock, picking away at the strings of his lute with studied concentration, humming along to his music. The moment he finished I was about to applaud and offer a few 'Bravos' when I noticed someone else.

Another ghost. But one I hadn't expected ever to see in the forest.

Ned?

Ned Bricklewick, one of my indoor-outdoor ghosts. Once upon a time he'd been a Victorian builder working around about East Devon. He'd died relatively young by today's standards, only in his late forties. He'd lived a hard life, working long hours in a tough occupation to earn a crust, and I think in the end he'd just been worn out.

Ned was dancing.

He'd bowed and swayed and stepped in time along to the music, pretending to have a partner at the end of his right arm. I won't say what I'd witnessed was of a professional standard. In fact I didn't imagine that Ned would be receiving a phone call from the producers of *Witches Got Talent* any time soon, but he had a certain masculine grace and lightness of touch that made watching him perform fairly painless. He'd obviously been practising.

A lot.

At that moment Mr Hoo, with his wide wingspan, decided to fly in from the clearing. As he negotiated the branches closest to me, he rustled the leaves and knocked a few twigs to the ground, scattering insects and leaves in his wake and thereby completely blowing my cover.

Ned looked up and clocked me there gaping back at him and, without a word, apparated away.

Luppitt grimaced. "Oh dear, oh dear!" he said, the White Rabbit to my Alice, and even as I began to ask him what he and Ned were up to, he'd followed Ned somewhere I couldn't go.

I tutted and twisted my head to stare up at Mr Hoo. "You did that on purpose."

"Hooo ooo." Mr Hoo denied it of course, the fibbing little ball of feathers and fluff.

Vance's booming laugh echoed around the marsh, and I ducked under his branches and scuffled through the undergrowth to join him.

"Young Alfhild!" he boomed. "How very good to see you!"

"You too, Vance," I said and waved. I didn't intend to jump into the water and give him a hug today. Now the music had stopped, I could make out the calls of dozens and dozens of toads and the rasping of crickets in the silence.

"How is everything at the inn?" he asked. "I hear you've had another spot of bother."

"Another murder." I nodded. "Yes. How did you hear about that?"

"Oh, I keep an ear to the ground." Vance shook his branches, and Mr Hoo flew up to sit with him. I folded my arms and gave the owl a hard stare. A right little gossipmonger he proved to be. "Ha ha ha!" Vance boomed again. "Actually, your great-grandmother came for a chat this morning."

"Did she?" I hadn't seen Gwyn for a while. Occasionally she went to ground and disappeared from the inn, and I wouldn't see her for days or even weeks on end. I didn't mind as long as she came back. Together we were like oil on water, and yet she was my greatest and strongest ally.

"Yes, we had a gay old time." Vance nodded. "I don't understand all this talk of film and television, and I'm not entirely convinced your great-grand-mother does either, but I have to confess it sounds like a fun gathering of people. Eat, drink and make merry is a good motto for life." Vance shook his branches approvingly.

"Not so much fun for Janice Tork-Mimosa," I said with a shrug. "But otherwise, yes." Changing the subject, I pointed at the rock where Luppitt had been standing and playing his lute. "You've had some entertainment this evening. Was that my Ned? Was he really dancing, Vance?"

"Wasn't it wonderful?"

I laughed. "I suppose so. He's a lovely fellow, always asking if I need anything, happy to turn his hand to everything. He never complains. Just gets on with being a really valuable part of my Wonky Inn Ghostly Clean-Up Crew." Ned helped with every-thing from maintenance to gardening (which he loved) to manning the bar (which he was less fond of). "But I've never seen him dance."

"Ho ho ho. He's learning! Ably assisted by Luppitt. You know, that Luppitt is such a talent. I do so enjoy the evenings when he and his brothers seek me out and play to me. My own personal concert."

"Right." I didn't mention they only played in the woods because I kicked them out of the inn. "Indeed, that's nice. But Vance?"

"Yes, my dear?"

I squinted into the shadows where I'd seen Ned. "He's such a quiet man. He never has much to say for himself at all. Just a shy smile here, a few words of smart-assery there." I had to confess to being stunned when I realised what he was doing here in the clearing. "Why was Ned dancing?"

"Why does anybody dance?" Vance asked, and I rolled my eyes as he became all philosophical on me. "Movement, like music, is life. An expression of freedom."

"Yes, but—"

"A tribute to those who have walked our paths before."

"I know, but—"

Vance laughed suddenly, a cracking explosion of sound, wood splitting and reverberating throughout the forest. "Or perhaps he's doing it for love?"

I stared up at the enormous tree in confusion.

Vance's eyes, large knots in the bark, blinked down at me in amusement. "It's an emotion you have experienced, young Alfhild," he reminded me in his kindly way.

"I have." I glanced around the edge of the pond, wondering where Jed was hanging out, and thought back to the time I'd turned both him and George into the toads they undoubtedly were. "But Ned?"

"Ned has a lady friend, I believe. Someone he is trying to impress. He's hoping to dance with her one day."

"Really?" I asked, and my heart fluttered in my chest. Ned was learning to dance in an Elizabethan style for a woman. How incredibly romantic. "Awww!"

"Hooo-ooo. Hoooo."

"Mr Hoo says you mustn't talk to Ned about it. He's rather bashful."

"Don't worry," I reassured them both. "Ned's secret is safe with me."

But who was the woman? Another ghost? Someone I knew?

I was itching to find out.

CHAPTER EIGHT

t just after twenty past five in the morning, the sun only just beginning to peep over the horizon, I found myself trying to munch on a piece of toast at the kitchen table. Monsieur Emietter and his entourage, minus Florence on this occasion, were busy preparing breakfast for the production crew. Bacon and sausages sizzled under the grill before being heaped onto silver serving platters and taken through to the dining area. No sooner had they been sent out than they were back again to be refilled.

Endless rounds of toast and bowls of eggs cooked in a variety of ways—poached, fried, boiled and scrambled—followed and again, just as quickly, the empty dishes were returned. We normally served breakfast at the inn from seven in the morning, but we'd agreed to start earlier, at a bleary-eyed 5 a.m., on the days when the crew were filming.

And that day had finally arrived.

The Great Witchy Cake Off would begin at nine today—amazingly on schedule in spite of the small issue of the murder of Janice Tork-Mimosa.

Florence's absence was noticeable, to me at least, because she was the one who kept me in tea and toast first thing in the morning when I hadn't really woken up. Without her I kind of felt aimless, unsure of what I should be doing or where I should be. I blinked at everyone coming in and out of the kitchen, wondering whether I should be giving them a hand and ultimately deciding they performed better without me getting in the way.

I drained my tea—made in a mug by me and not a patch on Florence's—and decided to take a walk in the grounds. The fresh air would clear my head and give me a renewed sense of purpose for the day. I exited the inn through the back door and wandered slowly around to my left. There were several temporary structures here, like portacabins, one of which acted as the wardrobe department, and one of which had been allocated to make-up. Through the open door I could see Mindi and Raoul sitting in leather swivel chairs being attended to by make-up artists wielding what looked like small paintbrushes laden with brown dust.

I continued on my way, grimacing at the thought of weighing down my skin with something that looked like emulsion paint, and couldn't help but overhear a conversation between two young women skulking around the corner.

"It's impossible," said the first one.

"You could lose your job," the other commiserated.

"Exactly!" The first woman sounded sorely aggrieved. "Why on earth is she even on the show?"

Oooh! I pricked my ears up and slowed down. Maybe they were bitching about Patty Cake and I could relay any pertinent information to George and his team.

"Who invited her?" asked the second woman.

"Someone who evidently doesn't know that you can't put make-up on a ghost."

Ah.

Giggling quietly, but actually empathising too, I picked up speed again until I was at the rear of the marquee. For the first time, I could see a number of cameras in situ, and members of the crew were preparing the area for recording. I shuffled to the door and peered in. One of the technicians, on her knees and placing small blue crosses on the floor using chalk, glanced up and smiled at me.

"Morning, Alf."

"Morning, Bertha. Busy already, I see." Bertha Crumb, a plain young woman of similar age to Charity, was employed as the floor manager. She wore her shoulder-length mousy-brown poker-straight hair tied back in a ponytail and could usually be found covered in dust or pushing a broom around.

"Oh yes. This is when the fun starts." She stood up and brushed the front of her trousers down.

"What are you doing?" I asked.

Bertha showed me the chalk. "I'm creating marks. This is where the judges will stand when the show begins, and there—" She indicated a set of red chalk crosses. "That's where Mindi needs to be." She pointed further away to where she had already marked out numerous crosses in green. "And that's where the contestants will need to stand while we film the opening of the first show."

"You'll interview them there?" I'd seen the show. One of the best things about it was getting to know the contestants and all their quirks.

"We do quick interviews in here for the opening, then we take them away—one by one—somewhere private. Usually to a nice place in the garden if the weather is fine. Then we ask them lots of questions. The interviews are spliced into the tape later."

"Oh, that's right," I said, fascinated by the process. Bertha returned her chalk to a small cardboard box. "Why chalk?" I asked. "Doesn't it rub off the floor quite quickly? Don't you have to keep re-marking the floor when it gets erased by people walking over it?"

"Ah!" Bertha winked and tapped her nose at the same time. "You'll have to wait and see, Alf. That is if they let you stick around while we film."

"Oh, I hope so!" I wriggled with anticipation. "I'm excited to find out what happens."

"Stick around then," Bertha instructed me. "Try not to get in the way. And maybe stay on Boo Sully's good side," she advised. "That works for me."

"I'll make it work for me too, then," I promised.

The eight contestants filed into the tent and took their places on lurid purple stools, including Florence, who didn't so much sit as hover in place. Two large cameras had been rolled into position to capture the whole of the marquee from the front, but there was an additional pair of mobile camera operators too.

The contestants had been trailed inside the tent by a group of make-up artists, who rapidly made finishing touches to make-up and hair while several technicians plugged in microphones and tested light and sound levels. As I'd already heard, Florence was causing an issue because the make-up artist couldn't powder someone who wasn't actually physically present.

I'd met everyone now. All of these contestants would be staying at Whittle Inn for the week-long shoot. They had a hectic schedule. By the end of the day, the judges would have decided on one person to eliminate. Then every day for the next four days one person would be knocked out until only three contestants remained. On the final day of filming there would be the ultimate *Cake-Off* final, and one person would become *The Great Witchy Cake Off* champion with the other two named runners-up.

Thrilling stuff!

With no sign of the judges or producers, or even Boo Sully, I watched as the assistant director, Jemima Clarke, took control. She issued a few final instructions to the contestants and one of the mobile camera operators snuck in for a close-up.

"Action," called Jemima.

"Rolling," responded a camera technician. To my amazement the cameras lifted off the floor, defying the laws of gravity. They floated in the air, making them lightweight and easy to move around. At the same time, the marks that Bertha had made on the floor disappeared, almost without trace. Instead, a slight coloured shine remained to mark the spots the judges, presenters and contestants would use during the week of filming.

Bertha caught my eye and winked. "Magick," she mouthed, then turned her attention to the set. "And in three, two, one," she counted in.

Jemima nodded at the first contestant. "Cue Hortense."

The first witch to speak to camera swallowed audibly. "My name is Hortense Briar. I'm a hedge witch living in the New Forest. I'm sixty-three and I have six cats." Flushed with nerves, she attempted a smile that looked more like a grimace.

"What are your cats' names, Hortense?" asked Jemima.

The question helped to put Hortense at ease. "Biffy, Squiffy, Belle, Scootch, Apple and Peach."

"Those are lovely names. Who's looking after them for you this week?" Jemima asked.

"My good friend Susanne." Hortense gave a double thumbs up to the camera. "Thanks, Susanne!"

Jemima nodded. "Just say your name one more time for me please, Hortense."

Hortense nodded, and this time her words flowed more naturally. "My name is Hortense Briar. I'm a hedge witch living in the New Forest. I'm sixty-three and I have six cats."

"That's a wrap," said Jemima and there was a ripple of applause. The first twenty seconds of filming were in the bag.

In rapid succession Jemima moved onto each contestant.

A tall black-haired witch with a thick accent, rather stunning to look at, went next. "Hello. I'm Jacinta Cadenza, originally from Espanola and now living in Brighton with my husband, Sergio. I'm thirty-eight and a sage. I love to paint abstract sea pictures in acrylics."

"Merry meet! My name is Eloise Culpepper. I'm a fifty-seven-year-old kitchen witch from Blackpool and I love to play poker." Eloise, with her long greying hair and prettily knitted cardigan, looked for all the world like someone Millicent would know from the WI.

The first gentleman to take a turn went next. "Hi! I'm Scampi Porthouse and I'm a founding member of the Blackdown coven. I'm sixty-eight and I play drums with a Mamas and Papas tribute band."

"Greetings. I'm Victor Wilde. A mechanical wizard from Swansea. In my free time I restore old Volkswagen Beetles."

"How old are you Victor?"

"Oh, I'm sorry, I forget for a minute."

"Can we go again please?"

And so it went. Davide McGulligan was the youngest contestant at just twenty-two, an apprentice mage from Glasgow. He seemed to be getting on well with Jemma Jackson already. Jemma, a twenty-six-year-old solitary witch from the Malvern Hills, professed to a huge love for everything Jane Austen related.

That left Florence.

"In three, two, one," repeated Bertha.

"Good morning to you. My name is Florence Fidler. I'm twenty-two years old and I'm a housekeeper from Whittlecombe in East Devon. I love people, all kinds of people, and watching my favourite programmes on television." She smiled happily into the camera, relaxed and confident.

"That's a wrap. Nicely done. We'll have to call you 'one-take Flo'," remarked Jemima.

"Take a breather everyone," Bertha announced loudly. "We're going to begin in earnest in about five minutes."

As soon as the camera operators downed tools, the make-up and wardrobe team were back, fussing and fiddling.

"Producers on set," announced Bertha, and a kind of hush fell as Boo led Patty, Murgatroyde, Faery Kerry and Mindi into the tent.

I had to step aside to let them pass. Hurriedly, I tried to melt into the shadows. Mindi brought up the rear—and what a transformation. Gone were the dry, grey hair and washed-out skin tone, the grubby creased clothing and bags under the eyes, and in their place was the Mindi I recognised from the television. Sleek, shining blonde hair and glowing skin, and a colourful silk shirt in bright green over white jeggings and rainbow sequinned slide-ons. Her make-up was perfect in every way, and not only did she appear ten years younger, but she also looked like she'd lost ten pounds and gained ten inches too.

I glanced around suspiciously. This could only mean one thing. The people working as make-up and wardrobe assistants were cosmetic alchemists, just like the one Wizard Shadowmender had sent me to in Bristol six months ago with the aim of turning me into Fabulous Fenella the Far-Sighted. Cordelia Denby had been her name, and quite a wizard she had been. I'd hardly recognised myself.

"Hmpf," I snorted, slightly disappointed that what I'd been served on endless episodes *of The Great Witchy Cake Off* had been an artifice. The beauty of it for me had been how kooky and natural the whole thing was. How much more of the show was purely staged for the cameras?

Boo Sully looked my way and raised his eyebrows. I smiled innocently and stepped further back into the canvas of the tent, hoping he wouldn't send me away. Behind him, Bertha wagged her finger at me. I folded my arms and assumed an air of nonchalance.

In an attempt to grab everyone's attention, Jemima clapped her hands like a schoolmistress. The contestants, nervous and excited, had been talking among themselves, loud enough that I could hear them ruing the gaffes they had made in their mini-introductions. Now they turned to Jemima expectantly.

"Boo is going to take over the direction very shortly. I want to thank you for your time so far this morning and wish you all the best. But first, Patty will launch the proceedings."

Oooh. This was interesting. I crept forwards again, intent on hearing everything she had to say.

Patty, dressed in chic black and white—and still wearing sunglasses, possibly in this case to protect her delicate eyes from the crazy amount of lighting in the marquee—held her hands up as though ready to conduct an orchestra. The tent fell completely silent. If I wasn't mistaken, most of us were holding our combined breath.

"As we begin to craft Series Sixteen of *The Great Witchy Cake Off*, I want us all to pause and remember an incredible woman. My good friend, Janice Tork-Mimosa."

Heads were bowed and we paid quiet tribute to the memory of the woman who had been murdered at the entrance to the marquee.

Eventually Patty looked up. "Wherever you are Janice, we miss you." She took a sharp breath, a cue to end the solemnity and get down to business. "On behalf of Murgatroyde, who is stepping into Janice's sensible shoes, Raoul, Faery Kerry, Mindi, Boo and indeed the whole of *The Great Witchy Cake Off* team, I would like to welcome the competitors to this iconic tent and wish all of you well." She peered through her dark glasses at the contestants on their chairs. "It is worth reminding you of the importance of fair play in the competition. To that end, unless otherwise stated on the day and during actual film-ing, you are forbidden from using magick either in your bakes or in any other capacity while inside the marquee."

She looked around at us all, her face deadly seri-ous. "To ensure all contestants abide by this, we set a no-magick zone within the confines of the tent. Bertha?"

Bertha reached into a cloth bag and pulled out a plain black wand with an ivory-coloured tip. She handed it over, somewhat reverently, to Patty, who once more lifted her arms and then, with a rapid flourish, sent out bright pink streaks of light that twirled through the air like lengths of ribbon, hitting the canvas ceiling and walls and ricocheting around, knotting together tightly to bind up the space.

I, of course, recognised a forcefield when I saw it.

Satisfied, Patty handed her wand over to Bertha, who tucked it back safely inside its bag.

"It only remains for me to wish all of you the very best of luck, and may the best baker win!"

A ripple of applause followed along with a few cheers, and Patty turned to have a few words with

Raoul before exiting the tent. I watched him watching her as she left. Bertha moved alongside me, sweeping up as she came, maintaining the cleanliness of the marquee for obvious reasons.

"Do you think they're having a fling?" I whispered when the floor manager was close enough to hear me, remembering how Raoul had seemed so keen to transport Patty back and forth to The Hay Loft. "A little illicit liaison?"

"I sincerely doubt that," Bertha snorted. "Patty bats for the other team."

"Patty's gay? Oh." That took the wind out of my sails. I'd assumed I was on to something. "It's just Raoul and Patty seem very close, that's all."

"Raoul is a lovely man. A bit of a charmer, I suppose. He's garnered a bit of a reputation in the past, but nothing overtly scandalous. There were rumours about him and Janice, but I don't know if they were founded on fact at all."

"Really?" I hadn't had an inkling of that, and I assumed that Florence—who let's face it had spoken about nothing else but *The Great Witchy Cake Off* and all who sailed in her for weeks and weeks—would have filled me in on that type of gossip had she heard such a thing. "Did you tell George—DS Gilchrist—that?"

"Unsubstantiated rumour and gossipmongering are really not my sort of thing, Alf." Bertha shook her head and resumed sweeping the floor around me.

"Fair enough," I answered. I had no such qualms about repeating what she'd told me though. George always insisted that intelligence about a crime, no matter how it had been come by, could prove invaluable. Ultimately the smallest piece of information could be used to break a case.

I skipped off to make a phone call.

"Welcome back to the *Cake Off* tent, where we're just six weeks away from unveiling the witchiest kitchen hostess with the mostest. Eight brand new contestants are here to pitch their skills to the nation. Who's got what it takes to create the ultimate magick in the *Cake Off* tent? Who needs to saddle up their broomstick and take the first flight out of here? It's all to bake for. It's back, it's more spellbinding than ever, it's *The Great Witchy Cake Off*!"

"Cut!" called Jemima.

"That's a wrap," Boo announced and smiled at the presenter. "Excellent, Mindi! Take a break everyone. We'll start again in twenty minutes."

"This is when they'll start baking?" I asked Bertha, who seemed to be the best person to answer all my questions. We were outside, the tent in the foreground, perfectly framed against Whittle Inn and the grounds. My wonky inn glowed brightly in the glorious sunshine under the bluest of skies. I'd brought down a trolley from the kitchen, loaded with a large urn and some coffee, tea and biscuits.

"Yes, at last!" Bertha laughed. "Now we get down to the nitty-gritty. They'll bake to a theme every day. Firstly a signature bake that will be similar for everyone. They have ninety minutes for that, then they'll have a technical challenge which can be anything between twenty and ninety minutes. Each judge takes a turn in choosing the technical challenge. It's lots of fun! Finally, they bake their show-stopper, which is entirely their own choice and should interpret the week's theme, and for that they'll have three hours."

"I remember," I said, thinking of all the programmes Florence and I had watched together in the attic. I wondered how she must be feeling. Excited? Nervous?

"The best part of the day is when we all get to sample the bakes." Bertha smiled.

"Mmm. That does sound pretty heavenly. What's the worst part?

"Bertha pulled a face. "Cleaning up. All the washing up. We have unlimited bowls and baking pans and utensils for the contestants to use, but the downside of that is all the clearing up that has to be done afterwards."

"The contestants don't do it?" I asked in surprise. I'd always rather assumed they would.

"Sadly not. It's down to us who work behind the scenes. It can take all night sometimes."

"Eww." I groaned in sympathy. Cleaning and washing up were my least favourite chores. Which was why I'd put my ghosts to good use in the past. "Oooh!" That gave me a thought. "You know what, Bertha? I might be able to help you out there."

CHAPTER NINE

Filming finished at around eight that evening, and Florence did not disgrace herself at all. In fact, I'd say she did quite well. She finished second in the first challenge, fifth in the technical and fourth in the showstopper, which meant that overall, she did well enough. Jacinta Cadenza became the first contestant to be sent home after her showstopper—described as 'slightly heavy' by Faery Kerry, and 'absolutely leaden' by Raoul Scurrysnood—failed to impress.

As soon as the cameras had stopped rolling and we'd all passed our commiserations on to Jacinta, I sent in a team of ghosts to help with the clear-up. They were their usual efficient selves, throwing plates, bowls, pans and cutlery around with studied insouciance, sweeping, mopping, spraying and scrubbing as though their very afterlives depended on it.

The remains of the day's baked goods were transported up to the inn and set up on some side tables, buffet style, in the bar for everyone to try after dinner proper. The contestants themselves looked absolutely exhausted, and a few of them decided not to hang around for an evening meal but to take the opportunity for an early night so they could prepare themselves for an even earlier start the next day.

Not so the technicians and production crew. I could see that many of them were ready to party till the wee hours, with one or two of them taking seats on stools at the bar and gleefully ordering cocktails from Zephaniah. Where did they get their energy from? I felt pretty exhausted and yet all I'd achieved during the day was observe everyone else work.

Given that most of my Wonky Inn Ghostly Clean-Up Crew were now engaged in cleaning down the contestants' kitchens in the marquee, and Florence had been excused normal duties for the duration of the filming, it fell to me to help out Charity by serving dinner to those who wanted something from Monsieur Emietter's menu, rather than Rob Parker's sausages (which I definitely fancied myself) so I ambled through to the kitchen for instruction.

Finbarr and his pixies were crowded around the kitchen table finishing up their supper before they headed out into Speckled Wood to patrol the perimeter. This was something we had been doing for nearly twelve months now. While the threat from The Mori had faded significantly after the skirmish we'd had during the summer, we'd decided that it was worth keeping up the patrols and keeping an eye on the sanctity of the forcefield we had in place to prevent encroachment by any enemies.

And besides, Finbarr was part of the family now. I'd miss his pale Irish face if he scurried back to the Old Country.

"Evening, Alf," he said in his broad Irish brogue.

"Hiya, Finbarr. Everything okay?"

"Absolutely fine and dandy." He speared a new potato and coated it in some sort of yellowy sauce. The contents of Finbarr's plate looked like pork loin in a mustard sauce with green beans to my untrained foody eye. Yum! I hastily reconsidered my previous desire for sausage and mash.

"That's good." I surveyed the pixies; there must have been a dozen of the little terrors. Half of them stared back at me with angelic eyes, the rest carried on devouring their dinners as though they hadn't been fed for weeks. "If you're still hungry later, you might find some cakes and pastries out in the bar." I wagged my finger at the pixies as a warning, all twelve of them gazing up at me with interest now. "But only after the guests have had their fill. Okay?"

"Yeah, that's right fellas. Let everyone else have their chance first," Finbarr chipped in and wiped his plate clean. The pixies grumbled amongst themselves and I tutted.

"Oh, by the way, Alf. I think Charity was looking for you. You have a new guest arrived, so it seems." Finbarr smirked and I frowned.

"A new guest?" I hadn't been expecting anyone. As far as I was concerned, the inn had been fully booked for the crew and contestants on the show. That's what I'd agreed to do. My stomach sank. Had I made a mistake and confirmed a reservation I shouldn't have done? I'd have to turn them away.

Cursing inwardly, I considered abandoning my idea of helping to serve dinner in order to head for my desk and investigate the booking, but Monsieur Emietter would be snowed under without me. There was nothing for it but to get the dinner service out of the way as fast as possible, or hope that the Ghostly

Clean-Up Crew finished quickly and came to my aid.

I grabbed a tray of potatoes and carved pork and headed back into the bar. Charity was coming the other way with her hands full of dirty dishes.

"Alf," she began as soon as she spotted me.

"I've heard," I said, not stopping to talk. "I'll get right to it as soon as we've finished service. I must have made a mistake."

"No, you don't understand—" Charity called, but I'd left her behind and found myself standing by the bar where Zephaniah was pouring a lurid pink cocktail from a shaker into a highball glass.

"Miss Alf," he called above the general hubbub of the busy room. There was a better atmosphere in here this evening; the shock of Janice's death had faded somewhat. I checked the ticket to see where my tray was heading. Table six. A small one nestled in the bay window. A lovely table for two that looked out over the front lawns, currently dominated by the marquee of course, but still a pleasant vantage.

"One sec," I replied, not wanting the food to get cold. I shimmied my way around the tables, following the route that took me towards the window.

I pulled up short as a familiar figure greeted me. "Alfie!"

"Silvan?" Surprise gave way to pleasure, but rapidly became something else. "What are you doing here?" I stared at his companion, awash with mixed emotions. I'd seen her before. By all that's green, she was stunningly beautiful.

"You remember Marissa?" he asked, and I did. His female 'friend'. That long hair, so blonde it was actually white, seemed to glow in the subdued lighting of the room. She wore a long silk sleeveless smock in a pale pink blush that complemented her colouring perfectly. She was tall and elegant, calm and unruffled. I stood in front of her looking like an omnishambles. But her pale blue eyes sparkled with warmth. However I felt about her, she obviously held no animosity towards me in return.

"I do," I replied as graciously as I could manage, trying not to let the words get stuck in my throat. "It's good to see you again."

"And you, Alfhild," Marissa replied, standing up and offering her hand.

I quickly deposited their tray of food on the table and shook hers. "Silvan talks about you all the time," Marissa said, and her laugh was a soft, merry tinkle that made me smile even against my better judgement.

"Does he?" I threw a suspicious look at Silvan and he raised one sardonic eyebrow.

"Hardly," he drawled. "I have many, *many* important things to think about, and I'm not sure you're one of them." His voice trailed away as he made a show of considering them all.

"Harumph," I snorted.

"This smells delicious." Marissa stepped in before I could respond with an acerbic putdown. Not that I'd managed to think one up yet.

Her gentle prodding about the dinner reminded me of who I was and what I was supposed to be doing. "Oh, you'll love this," I told her. "It's one of Monsieur Emietter's classics. He really does blend a fabulous mustard sauce, and it balances the pork and beans beautifully."

I served the couple quickly and efficiently. "Would you like anything else?" I asked, returning the empty serving dishes to my tray and checking they were alright for water. "Any wine?"

"Later perhaps," Silvan answered for both of them and his eyes twinkled with devilment. I badly wanted to smack him on the head with my tray.

"Just give Zephaniah a shout," I replied, anxious

to underline that I wouldn't be the one at the dark wizard's beck and call tonight. Then I swivelled on my heel and marched away, more than a little self-conscious about the clumsy figure I'd cut in comparison to the gorgeous and elegant Marissa.

Charity was still in the kitchen when I returned there with my empties. She took one look at my face and grimaced.

"Sorry, mate. I did try and warn you."

"I don't understand," I griped. "We're fully booked. Which room have you put them in?"

"We *were* fully booked," Charity explained patiently. "But don't forget we're a contestant down because Delores left and was replaced by Florence, and Florence doesn't need a bedroom."

Of course. That made sense. Plus Patty's room was free. We'd put Murgatroyde in Janice's old room. And tomorrow we'd have another room free because Jacinta Cadenza was heading home. I banged my tray down on the counter in annoyance. "Why didn't I know anything about the reservation?"

"To be fair, I didn't either." Charity straightened up the dishes on my tray. "It was a complete surprise when they turned up, but I checked, and the room *was* reserved for them." Our eyes met and a look of understanding passed between us.

"Gwyn?" I muttered.

"Undoubtedly."

"I'm going to have to have words," I said, annoyed that my great-grandmother always seemed to cave in to Silvan's requests so easily. "I don't know what she sees in him? Why does she like him so much?" I headed for the door to go in search of Gwyn.

"Why does anybody?" Charity called after me. "Handsome, intelligent, witty, devilish..."

"Oh, give over," I retorted over my shoulder.

"His girlfriend is pretty too," Charity added.

I slammed the door as I exited the kitchen.

Gwyn, of course, was nowhere to be found.

My great-grandmother had a terrible habit of leaving me in the lurch when I needed her. "I know you're around," I hissed as I closed 'our' bedroom door. "You just don't want—"

"Good evening, Miss Alf. Are you looking for me?" Florence apparated beside me, but for once she didn't have her feather duster with her. I wondered where she'd left it.

"Grandmama actually," I grumbled, but then

realised Florence was looking rather pleased with herself, and I was being a bore. "Hey! Congratulations, Florence." We exchanged air kisses—because you can't kiss a ghost—and I beamed at her. "I'm so proud of you! Everyone at Whittle Inn is rooting for you."

"Do you think I did alright, Miss Alf?" Florence asked, genuinely anxious.

"More than alright, I'd say! You made it through. Every day you get through will be magnificent. And remember"—I wanted to make sure she knew it didn't matter to us if she didn't bring home the coveted *Great Witchy Cake Off* trophy—"you'll always be our star baker, no matter what happens."

"Aww thank you, Miss. I appreciate that." She twirled lightly in the air. "Right, I'd better get down to the kitchen. I want to help Monsieur Emietter clean up, then I need to think about my bakes for tomorrow."

"I thought we agreed you didn't have to do any clearing up?"

"We did, Miss. But I want to practise my blood orange sponge tonight, so I want Chef out of the kitchen sharpish."

"Gotcha." I nodded. "If you see my grandmama, please tell her I'd like a quick chat."

"I will do, Miss!" Florence began to fade away. "Nice to see Mr Silvan again, though, isn't it? And his lovely girlfriend."

"Is it?" I asked in annoyance, but she'd gone, and I was grumbling to myself.

CHAPTER TEN

The sun had yet to rise by the time my alarm went off the next day. While the early starts were becoming slightly easier, I must confess that it was a secretly and insanely grouchy Alf who greeted the first guests with juice and a fry up.

By 7 a.m., everyone who'd wanted breakfast had grabbed some, and Charity and I were able to begin clearing up.

"What about Silvan and Marissa?" Charity asked me. "Should we leave a table set up for them?"

I pulled a face. "Not worth it. You know Silvan. He'll lay abed until midday if he can get away with it. He knows he can send down for a tray if he fancies anything."

As long as I wouldn't be the one taking it up to him.

The assumption, therefore, was that my non-

Cake Off guests were enjoying a lie-in, so finding Marissa returning from a walk a few minutes later was a surprise. "Am I late?" she asked in concern. "Is there anything left?"

"Of course, of course! Anything you like. Take a seat and I'll run and grab you some juice." I indicated the table she'd been seated at the previous evening and she settled down with a smile.

"Porridge," she answered when I asked her what she fancied, "with a little jam. And tea please."

When I brought her breakfast to the table, she gestured at the empty seat. "Won't you join me for a few minutes?"

I sat, feeling for all the world like I was just about to face some sort of Spanish inquisition, but Marissa merely smiled and spooned some raspberry jam on top of her porridge before dousing it all in milk.

"Your Speckled Wood is beautiful," she said in between mouthfuls. "You are so lucky to have access to your very own piece of forest. Walking in nature is something I dream about often." Marissa lived in Tumble Town, a cramped and overbuilt area of narrow lanes and old buildings located behind Celestial Street, populated by the underworld of the witching and wizarding community. "I'd have loved to meet Mr Hoo on my travels though."

Silvan had evidently mentioned my feathered familiar. "By all means go up and meet him after breakfast if you like," I offered and pointed directly above my head. "My rooms are on the next floor. He'll either be balanced precariously on my bedstead, hanging out of one of the windows, or he has a perch in my office.

"I'd like that. Is he friendly?"

Occasionally grumpy like his owner, I could have said, but settled for, "A complete flirt where our guests are concerned. I'm often worried that he'll go off with someone else."

"He never has so far. That's a good sign." Marissa laughed. I was struck again by what a warm and engaging person she was.

"What are your plans while you stay here?" I asked.

Marissa shrugged. "Some walking, some sight-seeing. Maybe catch a little of the filming if they'll let me."

"I'm sure they will. I'll have a word with Bertha, the floor manager. She's been very good about answering my questions and letting me catch a peep of all that's going on." I stood. "Speaking of which, I'd better get a shake on and make sure everyone has what they need."

"That would be wonderful, thank you, Alf. You are so very kind."

"You're most welcome. Catch you later. And say hi to Mr Hoo for me."

"Alf!" Charity called me as I began to climb the stairs heading for my office a little later. "Your mobile keeps ringing. It's down here." I headed back to the kitchen and plucked my phone from the kitchen table. Six missed calls from George.

Oooh! A breakthrough?

I quickly hit redial and listened to the buzz as the call rang through and then connected. "Alf!" George's voice sounded disembodied, or almost like he was talking to me from a cave. I could only assume he was hands-free in his car.

"Have you been trying to get hold of me?" Daft question. Of course he had.

"I'm on my way over to Whittlecombe now," he shouted. "Need to ask folk a few more questions. Including you."

"That's fine," I said. "Everyone expects the police to be in and out all week until all this has been cleared up."

"Sure." The line was atrocious, and although he added something else, I couldn't make it out.

"You're breaking up," I told him. "I need to go into the village now." I spoke loudly and slowly, hoping he would hear what I was trying to say.

"I'll meet you there," he said, and the line went dead.

I rolled my eyes. I would have to get a move on then. He was only travelling from Exeter, not the other side of the moon. He'd be there in twenty minutes.

I didn't bother changing, just kept the same robes on I'd been wearing during morning service. What's a bit of spilt egg yolk or baked bean juice between friends? Plus, the early start meant I hadn't yet had a chance to shower or put a comb through my hair. I wound my long curls around my fist and secured them into a messy bun on the top of my head, smoothed down my robes, grabbed my purse and trotted out of the inn and down the drive.

There was a certain coolness to the day, with a hint of damp in the air. We might have a little rain this afternoon, I decided. I skipped along the lane that led from Whittle Inn's drive to the marginally wider lane at the bottom leading into the village.

Whittlecombe was busy for the time of day. Mums

were coming home after dropping their children off at school, retirees were stocking up on groceries from Whittle Stores or queuing for pensions at the Post Office. I had a short list of things I needed from Whittle Stores and could be done and dusted in quick order, ready to meet George when he drove down the main street looking for me. I guessed we could grab a coffee.

In my haste to get everything done, I wasn't looking where I was going and missed the step when I dashed out of Whittle Stores. I'd probably have ended up flat on my face had it not been for someone grabbing my arm.

"Steady as you go," came a concerned voice, and I looked up into the nerdy but not entirely unpleasant face of Mr Bramble's son.

"Oh, thank you!" I exhaled in surprise. "Erm..."

"Alex," he reminded me helpfully, obviously realising I'd totally forgotten his name.

"That's right," I laughed self-consciously.

"And you're Alfhild. My parents' landlord."

"Yes," I replied. It seemed odd to hear such things said out loud. I still, even after twelve months, struggled to get used to the idea that I'd become a landlord, responsible for over a dozen properties and their tenants.

"Listen. Er..." Alex's face flushed the colour of late-season beetroot. "Forgive me if this is out of order. I don't really know anyone around here anymore. All my friends have moved away upcountry. I wondered if you would... ah... care to join me for a drink this evening?"

Taken aback, I found myself blushing along with him. Was Alex asking me on a date? Or was this purely because he didn't know anyone else our age? "That's a little difficult—" I started to say.

Alex widened his eyes, instantly mortified. "Because you're our landlord? Oh! I didn't think of that."

"No, no." I held my hands out to stop him. "Nothing like that."

"Oh. I'm sorry. It was very forward of me." He grimaced.

Poor Alex. I wished the ground would open up and swallow me. "No, it's just that—"

"You have a boyfriend?" Alex clasped a hand to his head.

"Alex! If you'll just let me finish."

"Sorry. I—"

"I have to stay close to the inn because we have some filming going on up there at the moment, and it would be unfair to take time away when the rest of my team are working incredibly hard—"

Alex shook his head. "Oh, I understand, I promise I do. I only meant The Hay Loft, but if that's not convenient, perhaps some other time."

The Hay Loft? I glanced over at the modern inn across the road where Patty was staying. I wracked my brains, trying to remember whether Lyle Cavendish had barred me from the hostelry itself, or whether that ban had only extended to the fields where the Psychic Fayre had been held. I chewed the corner of my lip, thinking.

"That's feasible," I said. "I must warn you though, I'm *persona non grata* over there, so we might have to do a runner."

Alex laughed and his face lit up. "How intriguing, Alf. Shall we say around eight-ish?"

"Sounds good to me."

I waited for George in the café. He'd obviously been held up somewhere, perhaps at roadworks. Gloria offered me a menu, but I decided to wait for my ex-fiancé to arrive. I took a seat at a table in the window so I could watch the world go by, my thoughts drawn to the reason George needed to speak to me.

Who had killed Janice Tork-Mimosa?

I pulled a serviette from the rack, dragged a pen from the pocket of my robes and started writing down names.

Rob Parker? I couldn't see Rob being a bad'un myself. All he cared about were his sausages. I'd been pleased to see that the production crew of *The Great Witchy Cake Off* had taken him to their hearts and stomachs, much as George and I had done.

I drew large question marks next to Faery Kerry and Mindi Blockweg. Neither of them seemed suspect to me, but it wouldn't hurt to do a little more digging, would it?

Raoul Scurrysnood. I underlined his name. If what Bertha had told me was true, Raoul had to be on our radar. A potential love affair with Janice. What had gone wrong? I'd passed that information on to George already and I wondered whether he'd been able to find anything out.

And what about Patty? Patty was hard work, and Janice had been working with her for years. The rumours—and there were many—suggested that they didn't see eye to eye on a large number of work-related matters. They say keep your friends close, but your enemies closer, don't they? Perhaps Patty had been the one who stuck the knife in Janice's chest.

I drew a picture of a cake knife on the serviette. Did the choice of weapon mean anything? Or had it merely been the closest thing to hand? The whole marquee had been full of items waiting to be put away in their proper places ready for filming.

"You're missing somebody important." George had arrived and stood alongside me, peering down at my scribblings.

"Who's that?" I asked.

"Delores Everyoung." He took a seat next to me and pulled the serviette in front of himself. "The contestant who found Janice."

"Do you think she's a suspect?" I'd forgotten all about her.

George shook his head. "Not really. She's been incredibly traumatised by the whole thing. One of my team travelled up to Gloucester where she lives. She's under the doctor and taking tranquillisers, the poor woman." He motioned Gloria over. "We haven't been able to establish any prior link between her and Janice."

George looked the menu over. "I'll have a bacon and egg sandwich, please, Gloria, and a large strong filter coffee, no milk thanks." He looked at me expectantly. "Have you eaten?"

Had I eaten? I'd been awake so long I couldn't remember. It would probably pay to make sure. "I'll have the same please. But tea instead of coffee."

"So? No solid leads?" I asked when Gloria had waddled back to the kitchen. She was an elderly lady with swollen ankles. I think she must have worked here at The Whittlecombe Café since she'd been a girl.

"Nothing," George frowned. "My team have checked and double-checked everyone's alibis. We have investigated every relationship we can think of between Janice and everyone involved in the production. I've spoken to all the staff—well, the human ones—at Whittle Inn. Assuming none of your ghosts committed the murder, which I'm guessing is a possibility I can't completely discount, then I'm now at a loss."

I pointed at the serviette. "What about Mindi and Faery Kerry?"

"According to Charity, they were coming down to breakfast. They were seen by several people and they can vouch for each other. And Charity, which is useful."

"As if Charity would lift a finger to hurt anyone," I scoffed. "She doesn't have a bad bone in her body."

"I know, I know!" George pacified me. "But I have to dot the i's and cross the t's—you know that."

I did.

Gloria arrived with our breakfast and I poured milk into my cup and stirred in a teaspoon of sugar. I needed the energy. I let the tea in its little teapot steep for a while longer.

George sliced into his sandwich and I watched the egg yolk ooze everywhere. I was going to need a bib, but given the current mucky state of my robes, maybe it didn't matter.

"Mmm." George took a bit bite of his sandwich and chewed thoughtfully before swallowing. "Do you know if there was anyone new in the village at the time of the murder?"

"Anyone new?" I tried to cut my sandwich into dainty quarters without making too much mess. This proved impossible. It seemed apparent that it had been an ostrich that had laid the egg now residing between the two thick slices of fresh bread on my plate. "Besides the two dozen or so who arrived for the filming of the programme, you mean?"

"No need for the sarcasm, Alf. It's most unbecoming."

I offered George my most scathing look and decided to attack the sandwich with a knife and fork. I definitely wouldn't be requiring lunch, that much was obvious.

"Well, you're talking about an enormous influx of people all at once," I pointed out.

"But nobody else?" George pressed.

I thought for a moment, staring out of the window, my fork poised in mid-air. A green MG shot past the window. "Lyle Cavendish's brother," I said.

"From The Hay Loft?"

"Yes, he's staying there. He's called Caspian. No. Crispin. That's his name."

George nodded and licked his fingers clean before pulling his notebook out of his pocket and making a note of that. "Crispin Cavendish. Anyone else?"

I hesitated, only for a fraction of a second, but George picked up on it instantly. "Alf?"

"Mr Bramble's son. You remember Mr Bramble? You resuscitated him at the Psychic Fayre."

"I do remember Mr Bramble. How's he doing?"

"Very well. Right as rain."

George nodded, pleased. "Great. So tell me about his son."

I licked my lips, a little nervous, a little bashful, a

little guilty. "He's called Alex. He's staying with his parents for a little while."

George studied my face. "Uh-huh." He waited for more, but I crammed a massive mouthful of sandwich into my gob and chewed viciously while avoiding his gaze. Unfortunately, Silvan and Marissa chose that moment to walk past the window. Silvan caught sight of me, stopped, and doubled over with laughter. When he stood up again, he made a passable impression of a hamster stuffing its cheeks.

I hastily swallowed my food and choked down a few mouthfuls of tea, cursing Silvan's timing. The next thing I knew, Silvan was leading Marissa into the café and heading towards us.

"By all that's green—" I grumbled, and then he was standing in front of us, Marissa smiling at the other customers and trailing in his wake. I abandoned my bacon and egg sandwich as a challenge too far.

"Fancy seeing you here, Alfie." Silvan smirked at me. "I was just saying to Marissa how sad I was that I'd missed you at breakfast and that I was feeling peckish, and look, here you are!"

"It's Alf, or Alfhild," I growled at him, but he ignored me and continued blithely on.

"And DS Gilchrist. I'm happy to see you again too!" He held his hand out and George shook it.

"Join us." George indicated the spare seats at our table then rapidly jumped to his feet as Marissa sidled up behind Silvan. I badly wanted to stab George through the hand with my fork, but nice witches don't do mean things. Instead, I smiled at Marissa.

"Yes, join us," I echoed. "Marissa, this is George Gilchrist. He's investigating a rather unfortunate murder. You might have heard about it." I wasn't sure whether the goings-on had made the news or not, but I rather assumed, given the media frenzy a few days ago, it probably had.

"You're a detective?" Marissa asked as George shook her hand.

"He's *the* detective," Silvan said in a nudge-nudge-wink-wink kind of way and I knew that he'd told Marissa all about George and me. I set my jaw and glared at Silvan with overt hostility.

He smiled and touched the side of his chin. "You have a little something—" he said to me, and cursing under my breath, I reached for a fresh serviette and wiped my face. Egg yolk.

"I really ought to be getting back to the inn," I

told George pointedly, but he was goggling at Marissa and hardly heard me speaking.

"You know what would be really lovely is if we all went out to dinner this evening," said Silvan as Gloria ambled up to the table to offer the newcomers her menus.

"Oh, that would be lovely," said Marissa. "Although I feel like I've done nothing but eat, drink and sleep since we arrived at Whittlecombe."

"That's all there is to do here," George chipped in.

Really? I thought. *Is that what you think?*

"Oh, that's a shame. I have a date already," I announced, trying to keep the triumph out of my voice. That would show them. Show them all.

"You do?" Now George was interested.

"Who's that?" Silvan asked, casually enough. "A new beau?"

Too late I realised I'd backed myself into a corner. "Nothing like that. Someone new to the area."

George appraised me with his clear blue eyes and understood straight away. Glancing down at his notebook, he asked me, "Alex Bramble by any chance?"

"He's just a friend. Not even a friend. I hardly

know him." My protest sounded weak. "We're just going to The Hay Loft for a drink." George's face was a picture. He stared at me with a look of total incredulity. He knew how much I hated Lyle and The Hay Loft.

"All the better!" Silvan clapped his hands. "Let's all go. We'll make an evening of it. George, why don't you bring Daisy—"

"Stacey," George and I both said at once.

"Stacey. Bring Stacey. Marissa and I will come along, and we'll all meet Alf's new *friend*. It'll be fun."

I jumped to my feet. "I really *have* to go!" I repeated. Right there and then, if I'd been a witch in less control of my faculties I'd probably have tried to turn Silvan into a cockroach. The problem was, he was more than a match for me, and he knew it.

Fury bubbled under my skin like a pan of sugar on the verge of caramelising.

Surprising then that when I glared at Silvan one last time before exiting the café, leaving George to pick up the bill, Silvan looked neither triumphant nor smarmy, only intrigued. His expression cooled the violence of my anger.

I knew exactly what he was thinking, I could

hear his voice as clear as a bell in my head. *Oh, those green eyes of yours, Alfhild.*

The contestants had started the day's technical challenge by the time George and I arrived back at Whittle Inn. We'd travelled back in his battered silver Audi and the silence had stretched out between us. I didn't feel the need to explain my 'date' with Alex, if that's indeed what it was, to a man who had cheated on me with one of his co-workers.

But I understood that if George was going to be able to carry out his work properly, then I needed to bury the hatchet, and for now, that shouldn't be in his skull.

Because the judges were barred from the tent while the contestants cooked, that meant that Raoul and Faery Kerry were hanging out in the bar. Charity had supplied them with some cups of tea, but they'd turned down a more substantial lunch on the grounds that within ninety minutes they would be required to blind taste the results of the contestants' baking.

George paused at the entrance when he spotted them. "I fancy a little informal chat with our judges if we can wangle a way to do that. Guards down, that kind of thing."

"Leave it to me," I said. "Give me a few minutes." I disappeared into the kitchen to arrange a few of Florence's cheesy profiteroles on a plate and then made my way back into the bar area.

"How is everything for you both?"

"Truly wonderful," gushed Faery Kerry. She seemed such a lovely gentle woman, it was a shame that she'd been caught up in all the dastardly deeds going on.

"Do you mind if I join you?" I asked her, and Raoul smiled up at me with those magnetic citrus-green eyes of his.

"Not at all." He half stood, and I hurriedly sat down and placed the cheesy profiteroles in front of me.

"You have to try one of these," I said. "In my opinion, these are amazing." I offered the plate and both judges took one each, more out of politeness than a desire to actually eat anything I assumed.

"Who made them?" asked Raoul nibbling on the top of his.

I had to lie. If I told them Florence had made them, it might have looked like I was trying to influence their decision making in her favour. "I did!"

"Well, they're really very good." Raoul finished his off and took another.

"I expect to see an application for *Cake Off* from you next year," Faery Kerry joked, and I laughed.

Never in a month of Sundays. There was no way this pair of judges would ever recover from having sampled any cake I'd made. The horror would live with them forever.

I popped a cheesy profiterole into my mouth and chewed ecstatically. They really were a taste sensation. If Florence didn't win this series of *The Great Witchy Cake Off,* I'd be very surprised.

"I think if I were judging these, I'd recommend using Roquefort cheese, for a hint of added tanginess. And maybe a little chervil..." Raoul Scurrysnood picked up another profiterole and turned it this way and that to get a better look at it from all angles.

I stopped in mid-chew. How could he criticise perfection?

"Mmm?" I swallowed. I didn't agree but I thought better of challenging him. I filed his comment as one more reason to be suspicious of the man, while George picked that moment to walk over.

"I'm just about done here, Ms Daemonne," he

told me and nodded politely at Raoul and Faery Kerry.

"Excellent," I said, and quickly held the plate with the remaining cheesy profiteroles out to him. "Why not take a seat and help us eat a few of these?"

"I really shouldn't." George played his part to perfection, pulling a chair out and sitting down before anyone could encourage him to leave. "There's a pile of work waiting for me at the station."

Faery Kerry nodded in sympathy. "Such wonderful work you all do. I have great admiration for the police."

"Thank you," said George and I thrust the plate closer to him. Yes, he'd just polished off a huge sandwich in the village but, right now, he needed to be acting the authentically hungry policeman, which he could do by eating even more. I sensed his reluctance as he took one of the pastry balls from the pile. "Yum."

Served him right. I smiled.

"Are you any closer to knowing what happened to Janice?" Raoul asked.

"I'm working on a few leads. It is difficult. She was a very private person." George took a mouthful of his profiterole. "Oh my goodness these are good. Did Florence make them?"

I kicked him under the table. "No," I said firmly. "I did."

George almost choked, and I kicked him again for good measure.

"Janice was a private person, that's true. But always kind," Faery Kerry was saying. "I can't believe she ever upset anybody enough for them to want to murder her. So sad. I feel sure it must have been a random occurrence. Perhaps a thief?"

George nodded as though he was giving this notion serious consideration. "What do you think a thief might have been after in the *Cake Off* tent, Ms Kerry?"

"Well I really don't know." The old faery looked confused by the question. "What do people like to steal these days?"

"The same as they always have, I suppose," I answered. "Money, jewellery..."

"Did Janice have much in the way of money or jewellery?" George asked.

Raoul was the one to answer this time. "Nothing particularly ostentatious. A couple of nice rings and a gold necklace her parents gave her for her eighteenth."

George wrote that down in his notebook and reached out to take another profiterole. "It sounds like you knew her quite well, Mr Scurrysnood. I hadn't realised that was the case."

Raoul startled me then. His pale green eyes, normally so flirty and all-knowing, suddenly brimmed with tears. "I'm sorry," he replied, his voice hoarse with emotion. "I didn't mention it before. I probably should have done."

"Mention what exactly?" George probed gently, knowing exactly what was coming.

Raoul cleared his throat. "Janice and I did have... a little something."

"A relationship?" George asked, and Raoul nodded. "How long did this go on for?"

We all looked expectantly at Raoul. "About six years."

"Six years?" Faery Kerry gasped. "But no-one else knew?"

"We didn't want anyone to know. And besides, it was on and off." Raoul shrugged.

George wrote something in his notebook. I imagined it said something like, 'volatile six-year relation- ship.' "It wasn't merely a fling though?" he asked.

Raoul laughed, a hollow sound and sat back on his chair to stare at the ceiling and remember the past. "No. Not a fling. Although... I feel that's all it ever really should have been. It started out as just one of those things. We were sharing a hotel. We rubbed along nicely. The evenings can be a bit boring while you're filming the show. It kind of just... happened."

"And kept happening for six years?" I chipped in, and George shot me a look that quite clearly told me to shut up.

"On and off," Raoul repeated. "On and off."

"And were you still an item when she died?" George asked.

Raoul shook his head sadly. "No. We broke it off a few months ago. For good." His face was blank, his voice flat. He did sound final about it.

"Why?" I asked, getting the question in before George could.

"I received a tip-off from someone that she was seeing someone else."

Faery Kerry and I gasped in surprise. Only George retained his cool. He'd heard it all before, of course. Not from Raoul obviously, but a similar story on other occasions. Illicit love affairs, betrayal and vengeance. That was his day job.

"Was she seeing someone else?" George kept his voice low-key, but I sensed the importance of the answer.

Raoul hesitated, swallowed and shrugged once

more. "To be honest... I don't know. Initially I thought she was... but Janice denied it on numerous occasions... and then she washed her hands of the whole discussion. She refused to talk with me about it."

"She took umbrage?" George asked.

"I'm not surprised," said Faery Kerry. "Did you have any proof?"

Raoul leaned over the table and placed his head in his hands for a moment. "I thought I did."

George frowned. "What do you mean?"

Raoul pulled his mobile phone from his pocket and lay it on the table, nodding at me. "You'll understand what I'm getting at, Alf." He squeezed the side of the device and the screen lit up. I was sent a series of emails, suggesting Janice was having an affair with Pierre de Corduroy. At first I dismissed them as a stupid crank by some deranged *Witchy Cake Off* fan, because we get plenty of those."

Faery Kerry nodded in agreement. Raoul flicked through his screens. "But then emails began to appear that contained video links. Normally I wouldn't have given them the time of day, in case they contained a virus or something, but one day, one started to autoplay and quite clearly it was Janice."

"With another man?" George asked.

"Yes."

"Can I see them?" George asked.

"No," Raoul said, and his reply was emphatic. "Not because I'm being difficult but because they disappeared the day she died."

"Disappeared?" George asked and I could hear the scepticism in his voice.

"I didn't delete them if that's what you're thinking."

George held his hand out for the phone. "A member of my team can check the call and email history and recover lost material." He emphasised the word lost, and Raoul looked at me.

I placed my hand gently on George's arm. "You won't find anything, George. Not if magick has been used to remove all traces."

George looked down at the phone and then at me, his lip curling in frustration. "Why can nothing ever be simple with you people?"

"Your people won't find any trace of anything—messages, photos, texts or calls on that phone," I explained. "Not if it's been removed with magick." I folded my arms. "Fortunately, *my* people will."

CHAPTER ELEVEN

"Everything alright, Florence?" I asked.

My housekeeper, generally so effervescent with excitement, seemed positively muted this evening. She'd come to find me after filming had finished to let me know that she had made it through day two and that the wizard Victor Wilde was on his way home.

I had taken a seat at my dressing table to make a valiant attempt at de-frizzing my freshly washed hair in an effort to appear sleek and elegant for my 'date' this evening. Ah yes, that intimate occasion with Alex Bramble... and Silvan, Marissa, Stacey and George.

What a crazy situation to find myself in. Silvan had a lot to answer for.

So preoccupied was I in attempting to straighten my crazy curly hair that I almost forgot to listen to her reply, but I caught the words, "I think I'll have to give up." Frowning, I turned around.

"I'm sorry. What did you say?"

"I'm just not sure I have the skills necessary to progress much further in the competition, Miss Alf. I was in the bottom two of the technical challenge this morning." Poor Florence. The worry on her face told me how much this competition meant to her.

"Oh, honey. I'm sure you do. You're the most amazing baker I know. Why just this afternoon I passed off some of your cheesy profiteroles as my own, and Raoul Scurrysnood absolutely loved them!"

"Did he?" Florence's little face perked up. "What did he say?"

"Erm…" Did I tell the truth, or did I sugar-coat it? I opted for the truth. "He loved them and said he would use Roquefort cheese with a little bit of chervil." I pulled a face, waiting for an explosion of indignation or tears of despair, but none came. Florence pondered on what I'd said for a moment.

"He likes tastes that are quite defined, doesn't he? Mr Scurrysnood? Clean, but specific." Florence's mind worked overtime as she processed what I'd said. "That's useful to know, Miss Alf. Thank you."

"You're welcome," I replied, admiring her mature approach to Raoul's critique, and turned back to the mirror to fuss over my hair again. When she fell silent once more, I fixed my gaze on her via the mirror. "What's up?"

"The theme for tomorrow is Victoriana."

"Victoriana? What's that when it's at home?"

Florence examined her nails. "They don't really tell us. They just give us the theme." She sounded despondent. Maybe she was out of ideas.

"But you were Victorian, Florence. I mean, when did you die? Eighteen-something?"

"1887. I remember it well."

I grimaced. I'm sure she did. "So, why not make sure your bakes are something to do with everything that was going on at the time?" I said, aware of how ridiculously vague that sounded.

"Because I don't know what was going on at the time," Florence said, and I could hear the exasperation in her voice. "I was a housemaid, saving up for my wedding. I lay fires and I beat rugs and I prepared tea for Mrs Daemonne, and I had two half days off per week and a full day once per month. I went to school until I was twelve and then I entered service. I occasionally read the newspaper when I prepared the fires, but other than that and the occasional dance I attended in Whittlecombe village hall, I can't say there was much going on in my life, Miss Alf!"

Silence.

I appreciated the problem. Victoriana could only be defined by those who viewed it from a distance, not by those who had vaguely inhabited an epoch whose greatness probably passed them by thanks to the sheer exhaustion of trying to survive.

But here was a problem I could help with. "Here's what we're going to do, Florence," I said thoughtfully. "I do have to go out now—as much as I'd like to give this entire evening a miss—but I'll try and get back as soon as it is polite to do so. Then I'll meet you either here or in the attic and we will have a think."

"You don't have to do that, Miss Alf," she protested.

"Of course I do. You're always helping me with life's little challenges, so I'm going to help you with yours. Maybe we can google some ideas."

"Wouldn't that be cheating, Miss Alf?"

"It would be cheating if you did it inside the marquee, but surely it can't hurt to do some research the night before? You can't tell me that the other five contestants aren't huddled over their mobiles and laptops in their rooms this evening?"

Florence grinned mischievously. "I could always go and take a look, Miss." She could, of course, by simply poking her head through the walls and doors.

"Let's not stoop too low," I reprimanded her, with a quick smile. "Don't worry. We'll come up with something. Right now, I'd better finish getting ready."

"Thank you, Miss Alf." Florence floated towards the door. "You're not really going to wear your hair like that though, are you?"

I purposely slipped out of the inn before Silvan and Marissa were ready to leave. Apart from anything else, I needed to explain to poor Alex that the evening had been hi-jacked rather, and we would be joined by my ex and his girlfriend, and another pair of witches—one of whom was a complete pain in everybody's posterior.

I wandered down Whittle Lane and dawdled outside the row of pretty cottages, waiting for Alex to come out of Ash Cottage where his parents lived. Of course, I couldn't fail to attract the attention of others, including dear old Millicent. First she stared at me through her front window and waved me in, then when I refused she came to the door, Sunny and Jasper rushing out to meet me, barking in excitement.

"I thought that was you. What are you up to?"

"I'm ah... meeting Alex Bramble. We're going for a drink."

Millicent appeared taken aback. "A drink where? The Hay Loft?" I nodded and tried not to scowl. "You must be desperate," Millicent chuckled, then taking a step closer to me so she could check out my face, she asked, "Is that lipstick?"

"Oh hush, Millicent. You really are evil." I gave her a warning look, but she only laughed again.

"With Alex though? He's not really your type, is he?" Millicent crinkled up her nose.

"I'm not planning on marrying him. I just agreed to have a drink, that's all." Millicent nodded but I could see scepticism in her eyes.

"Evening, ladies!" From across the road came a cheerful shout. We turned to see Sally, wearing a short flowery dress and a pair of high heels tottering towards the entrance of the pub.

"Looks like Lyle will have a full house tonight," Millicent said and beamed back at Sally as she waved at us.

"Is she seeing Lyle's brother again, then?" I asked

in a whisper. Not that Sally could have heard us now that she was safely inside The Hay Loft.

"They've been everywhere together over the past few days. Never out of each other's company." Millicent frowned. "I don't like it. Sally's had a rough time in the past; she deserves someone better."

"Hi." A small polite voice from behind us startled me and I whirled about.

"Alex," I said. "Hi." I nudged Millicent with my elbow. "You remember Alex."

Millicent snorted. "Of course I do. Well, I'd best get on with my spinstering," she said. "Do have a lovely evening, you beautiful young things." She smiled at Alex, winked at me and then whistled to the dogs. They trotted into the cottage and she closed the door quietly.

Alex and I stood looking at each other, neither of us quite knowing what to say.

"I suppose we should—" Alex gestured at The Hay Loft and I nodded.

"Yes, we should." I led the way across the road and into the lounge bar. Unlike Whittle Inn, it was a modern bar, made to look old but in a very clean and stylised way. There were lots of white walls, clean wooden surfaces and mirrors. But if you looked more closely, you could see the veneer everywhere; nothing was solid, nothing as it appeared.

Alex pointed at a small table for two in the corner, intimate and invitingly close to the fire.

"Oh," I said and pulled a face. "Don't hate me, Alex, but I was rather steamrollered this afternoon into inviting a few other people." I'd expected Alex to be disappointed, so was rather perturbed when this news raised a smile.

"Really?" he asked. "That's not a problem. Will a table for four do?"

"Make it six," I said, and we found one on the other side of the room. We settled ourselves and were about to make a decision about what to drink when George walked in, Stacey holding onto his arm. I couldn't decide whether this was a possessive or a defensive gesture on her part but found myself despising her either way.

And that awareness of my emotion made me miserable. Why should I care? What was George to me now except ancient history? We'd made our beds. Separately.

I did the introductions, and Stacey hastily sat next to Alex. I guessed he was a safer bet than me, the mad old witch lady who'd once turned her new beau into a toad. Alex and Stacey struck up a conversation—about work of all things—as George slipped onto the bench next to me.

"How's it going?" he asked. "Did you pass on our request?"

"I made the phone call," I replied, aware we sounded like a couple of Cold War spies.

"And?"

I placed my hands on the table firmly. "Tomorrow."

He nodded. "Good. What are you drinking?"

"Greetings, one and all!" Silvan, clad head to toe in black and wearing a black silk cloak to boot, burst through the door in a sudden explosion of energy. The other customers—and to be fair there were a few of them tonight—turned around to see who was making all the noise. Silvan waved merrily, wafting his arms around in a most melodramatic way, and everyone immediately pretended to mind their own business. It was all frightfully British.

"Are we late?" Silvan boomed. "I'm so sorry. Entirely my fault, it takes me an aeon to lace these boots." He shook George's hand, and then Alex's when I introduced them. "Ah, the lovely Stacey," Silvan cooed and gently raised her hand to his mouth, brushing a kiss over her knuckles. She blushed a pretty shade of rose. He then turned about and pulled Marissa into the circle. Dressed all in white, she appeared the very antithesis of Silvan. Calm and contained, as tall as him and glowing with a glorious luminosity, she drew admiring looks from all who laid eyes on her.

Including both George and Alex.

I realised I might as well not have bothered dressing carefully or spending an hour trying to tame my hair. Between these roses—the illustrious Marissa and the dewy youth of Stacey—I was a mere thorn. My stomach rolled with a pang of regret, but I quickly bit that negative thought in the bud. Under the table I squeezed my nails into the palms of my hands and reminded myself of all I had and all I was. A businesswoman, a ghost whisperer, a warrior, a witch. When I looked up again, I had renewed my sense of worth and regained my equilibrium. I felt strong.

Silvan met my eyes for a brief moment, and a little smile played on the corners of his mouth—not of amusement, not mocking me: more appreciative than any of those somehow—but I hardly had time to decipher what I saw there because in the next second he was teasing me for my wild hair.

I ignored him and stood, intending on assisting George at the bar if he could ever manage to tear his eyes away from Marissa. "The drinks, George?" I prompted him when it looked like he had no intention of moving.

"Oh yes. What's everyone having?"

I waited at the bar while George checked and double-checked what everyone wanted. I spotted Sally with Crispin at the opposite end of the room and tried to catch her attention, but she was leaning into Lyle's brother, hanging on his every word. His hand played lazily with a lock of her hair, but I noted that when she spoke to him at any length, his eyes flicked away, looking at the other women in the bar and dining area, occasionally alighting on Marissa and sometimes on Stacey. The man was a player. A bubble of annoyance bloomed in my chest. How could he be so cavalier with poor Sally's affections?

I'd have to report this back to Millicent. She was right, we needed to do something.

Of Lyle there was no sign this evening, and that pleased me. With any luck I could relax and enjoy a couple of hours with my friends. But as I carried a couple of glasses of wine back to our table, I couldn't help but reflect on what an odd bunch we were. A dark witch, a detective, a whatever-kind-of-witch Marissa was, me... and two ordinary mortals, one of whom had no knowledge of who or what we were.

The table had been re-jigged, I noticed. Alex had seated himself next to Marissa. George slipped into the space between Marissa and Stacey. Stacey wanted to be close to Silvan, so I ended up between Alex, which was fair enough... and Silvan. As I lowered myself onto my chair, Silvan grinned at me. "Well, this is nice," he said.

I turned my back on him and tried to engage Alex in conversation. This proved difficult because Alex and Marissa were involved in an avid discussion about old cars. Classic vintage cars to be precise. I knew nothing about cars so couldn't imagine how to contribute to the conversation. I tried to appear interested, listening as their discussion progressed to alternate energy sources for vehicles, but gave up. Taking a large slug of my wine I turned about to talk to Silvan, but he and Stacey were discussing anatomy with George. Stacey appeared agog at Silvan's ability to name every bone in the human body.

Of course he can, I wanted to say. He's a necromancer. But I can't imagine how that might have gone down at our little dinner party, so I kept my tongue in check and concentrated on my wine instead.

And that was pretty much how my 'date night' panned out.

I managed to enjoy some conversation with Alex, but clearly his interest lay with Marissa. I had a feeling George struggled too, but at least Stacey lavished her affections between both George and Silvan. For his part, Silvan lapped up all the attention Stacey doled his way, knowing full well he'd be heading back to Whittle Inn with Marissa.

From my vantage point as chief wallflower, I spotted Crispin and Sally when they departed quite early on. They hadn't eaten, just enjoyed a drink at the bar. I wondered briefly where they were off to and reminded myself to chat to Millicent about what, if anything, we could do with regards to Sally's predicament.

For all we knew, Crispin was nothing like Lyle and I was doing him a disservice. But my intuition said otherwise, and I wasn't one to dismiss a gut feeling.

I waved goodbye to George and Stacey with some relief. We'd congregated outside Mr Bramble's cottage as we tipped out of the pub at closing time. It had gone eleven and I needed to be up before five. If I hurried up the lane—leaving Silvan and Marissa to dawdle along behind me—then I could have a quick bath and still manage five hours' sleep.

"Thanks, Alf. I've had a wonderful night and you have lovely friends. We must do it again," Alex said, kissing me on the cheek. I smiled politely.

"Yes, yes, we must!" I hoped I sounded earnest enough and tried not to break into a run as I hotfooted it out of the village, away from the muted streetlights, along the dark lane towards home. I'd obviously overdone the wine because I struggled to walk in a straight line, but it made no difference. At this time of night there was little if any traffic. I could have lain down and taken a nap and probably not been disturbed until the milkman rattled his bottles as he drove into Whittlecombe in his electric van just before daybreak.

It felt good to be free from the noise and stuffiness and sheer fakery of The Hay Loft. Free to enjoy the breeze, alone and unencumbered.

"Relationships are so complicated." I tried to articulate my thoughts and feelings out loud as I went, ambling up the lane towards the drive of Whittle Inn, my voice sounding a little thick with the alcohol.

"I don't know if George and Stacey are happy." I shrugged dramatically into the shadows. "I can't tell.

Does George like Stacey? Does Stacey like George? Stacey likes Silvan." This last thought grumbled out of my chest.

I hiccoughed and chortled. "She must be mad."

For some reason that made me laugh out loud. Hysteria gripped me, until I was howling in mirth and doubled over at the side of the lane, leaning against one of the old oak trees sheltering the drive.

I heard footsteps behind me and straightened up quickly, trying to ascertain whether there was any danger, but the soft glow of Marissa's pale shift lighting up the darkness quelled my sudden fear.

"Are you alright, Alf?" Marissa's gentle voice drifted out of the shadows.

"M'fine," I said, and tried to stand up straight. Silvan's low, knowing chuckle floated through the darkness.

"Do you need a hand?" Marissa asked, coming alongside me and reaching out, her cool touch landing on my wrist.

"M'noooo." I shook my head, the vehement denial of the woman who has overdone it. "M'fine. Thanks though."

Silvan joined us and nodded at Marissa. "You go on. I'll see you in the bar for a nightcap."

"A nightcap sounds good," I said as Marissa

drifted away, waiting for Silvan to tell me I'd had enough, but he didn't, so I couldn't argue with him.

"Let's get some more air," he said. "Walk with me."

"I don't want to walk."

"Then don't," Silvan shrugged, easy either way. He moved off, heading away from the inn and towards the gardens and the marquee. I could see lights in the tents and trailers at the edge of the grounds. Some of the production crew were still up. In fact, some of them were probably still working.

I swayed where I was standing and hiccoughed again. It probably was best I have a little more air before heading inside for my bed.

"I was going to take a bath," I said, more to myself than anyone else.

"You'd more than likely drown yourself," Silvan called back and continued on his way. Glowering at his back, I hurried after him until I'd caught him up, but as I swaggered alongside him I nearly lost my balance. I reached out and grabbed his arm.

"I don't want to hold your hand," I explained to him. "It's just the world seems to be on a tilt tonight."

Silvan coughed. "I completely understand, Alfhild." He didn't shake me off, just left my hand where it was and continued to walk slowly around the outskirts of the grounds. To our right, I could see the uninterrupted ribbon of energy that made up Whittle Inn's forcefield. Finbarr and his pixies were out there somewhere. That gave me a sense of wellbeing.

Thoughts tumbled around my head. George, Stacey, Silvan and Marissa. Alex.

"He's not right for you, you know?" Beside me, Silvan kept his eyes facing front and his tone mild.

"Who?"

"Alex."

How had he known I was thinking about Alex? I thought about protesting. After all, what business was it of Silvan's whether the man was right for me or not? We'd been on one non-date, and it had been Silvan's fault that a coach party of onlookers had accompanied me, when really it should have been Alex and I, just getting to know each other a little better.

But I didn't object because I knew he was right. "I wasn't intending to settle down and have his babies," I grumbled.

Silvan snorted. "That's alright, then."

The cheek of the man. I stopped and scowled at him, badly wanting to put him in his place, but unconcerned, he kept moving away from me, continuing his walk. I ran after him. "Why did you come?"

"I thought it would be nice if we all went out and had dinner together. And you have to admit, we had fun. I enjoyed getting to know George and Stacey a little better."

"That Stacey would certainly love to get to know *you* a little better," I retorted.

Silvan glanced at me and grinned. "I know." He walked on. "Well, *we* had a good time. It was only you who didn't."

"You put me in an impossible situation," I complained. "Why would I want to go on a date with my ex and his new girlfriend?"

"Why does it matter? If you don't want to be with either of them?" Silvan asked. You couldn't fault his logic.

I snapped. "That's not what I meant anyway. I wasn't talking about the date-that-wasn't."

"What then?"

"I meant why did you come *here*? To the inn? With your girlfriend? Are you deliberately—"

"Deliberately what, Alf?" Silvan finally stopped walking and turned about, edging closer to me, until his face was mere inches from mine. The warmth of his breath fanned across my skin.

My thoughts tumbled over and around themselves. "Deliberately—" I searched for some semblance of rationality in my muddled mind, but nothing came. What was he doing here? Why had he come? Was he trying to make me jealous?

Jealous? Absurd! Why should I be jealous?

Silvan's eyes glittered and he raised his hand, as though to brush the hair away from my face.

From up ahead came the sound of a trailer door slamming. It made me jump. We both looked that way. Silvan cocked his head and narrowed his eyes.

"What is it?" I whispered, reaching out with my own senses, but in my confuddled state I found myself touching the energy of those asleep or lounging around in the trailers, unable to discern friend from foe. Confused, I pulled myself back in. "Is there something to be worried about?"

Silvan reached into his robes and pulled out his wand. "Why don't you have your wand with you, Alfhild?" he asked me, and I automatically put my hand to where it would be. But I wasn't wearing my robes and I hadn't brought my wand out with me.

The realisation that I could have been here alone and defenceless hit me like a shedload of bricks, sobering me up rather sharply. Silvan gestured for me to stand behind him, and then moved forwards. I followed him closely, my hands loose by my side. I was ready to attack using the methods I'd always used, until the day Silvan had begun to teach me the dark arts and new ways to defend myself, and I'd found a chunky piece of Vance in the marsh and forged my own wand.

I didn't need to sense Silvan's disapproval; I was disappointed in myself. I should have been ready for all potential situations. I'd let myself down, and I, of all people, knew at what cost that could come to my beloved Whittle Inn.

"I've been complacent," I said, and turned my head slowly to look over at the marquee, remembering Janice lying in the entrance there with a cake knife buried in her chest.

We crept forwards, our footsteps silent as we crossed the lawn. Silvan twisted this way and that, trying to get a lock on whatever it was that had alerted him to something not quite right. He followed a trail I couldn't see that led to Rob Parker's sausage van, now dark and closed up for the night.

Or so it seemed. We circled the van slowly, and at first glance everything did seem normal, but when I reached out to try the door, Silvan touched my hand with his wand and silently shook his head.

Instead, he illuminated the tip of his wand and

tapped lightly on the door. It swung slowly open, the wand's beam casting shadows around the interior. Nothing obvious to see, and just the faint scent of fried onions and cleaning products. Everything was spick and span, the way Rob liked to leave it after a day of selling his products.

I took a breath, relieved that we hadn't found anything, just as something—a missile—shot out of the van and through my legs, spinning me around and knocking me to the floor. I was far too slow to get a good view of it, or even watch it as it made a bid to escape. Not so Silvan, however. He flicked his wand. "*Stupefaciunt*," he ordered, and the thing, already a good twenty metres away from us, heading for the marquee, stopped dead and keeled over.

I jumped to my feet and followed Silvan as he raced across the lawn, but he hadn't banked on the guy lines. Unable to see them in the dark, he stumbled over the first one he made contact with. Following so closely behind, I had to try and leap over him. In my slightly inebriated state, I made a mess of it, stood on his leg and ended up pitching headfirst on top of him.

I lay stunned where I was for a moment, trying to catch my breath, looking over at the grey lump still on the ground near the entrance to the marquee.

"I knew you'd fall for me one day," Silvan said from beneath me, and I hurriedly rolled off him and groaned.

"Ow."

Silvan pushed himself up, heading for the thing, but he hadn't taken more than half a dozen steps when a pulse of magickal energy exploded, and the creature—whatever it had been—vanished from our view.

We scurried over but we were far too late. It had gone. Whether it had been banished or destroyed, there was no way of knowing. Silvan waved his wand around in the general area.

"A djinn," he said. "I haven't come across one of those for many a year."

"A djinn? What's that?"

"It's a spirit that can take the form of a human or animal. Some witches conjure them to do their bidding. Especially useful if you're up to no good because you can send them out to do your evil deeds rather than risk being caught or hurt yourself. Tumble Town used to be overrun with them, but there was a crackdown and many of them have been cleaned up. It's a neat little trick to harness one though. I'll have to show it to you sometime."

I wasn't sure that was such a good idea. It was

hard enough managing all the ghosts that flocked around me all the time, let alone a bunch of evil djinns.

We stood back to back, turning around and scouring the dark grounds, peering into the blackest of shadows, searching for anything out of the ordinary.

"It's no good," Silvan said. "There's nothing left to see here. We might as well head to bed."

"We'll have another look in the morning," I agreed.

"Starting with Rob's van," Silvan told me. "You go on. I'm going to secure it for now."

"Okay," I said. "Goodnight."

"Goodnight."

I watched Silvan walk back to Rob Parker's van.

Rob Parker *again*?

That's just a coincidence, I thought to myself.

Surely?

Not quite midnight. I figured a bath was now out of the question. Reluctantly I reset my alarm ten minutes earlier. I'd take a shower first thing instead.

I plonked myself down on the edge of my bed, just about ready to collapse.

"Miss Alf?" A plaintive little voice called me from the doorway. A pair of worried eyes stared out at me; a faint tinge of singed cotton danced beneath my nostrils.

Florence.

I'd completely forgotten I'd promised to help her. I wanted to tell her we'd do it tomorrow, but tomorrow would be too late. Tomorrow she needed to bake, and it needed to go well for her.

So instead of snuggling down beneath my quilt, I blinked at her with tired eyes, my head still woozy from all the wine. "Oh, Florence. Sorry I'm so late. If you make me a cup of tea and join me in the office, we'll make a start."

As Florence apparated away, I called out to my great-grandmother. "Grandmama. I really need your help." I thought of Florence, and Janice, and Silvan and George, and how complicated my life was. "In so, so many ways," I added.

Just after one in the morning and I was still brainstorming the notion of what Victoriana might mean.

I was writing our ideas down on a large sheet of paper, while Gwyn and Florence flitted around the room at varying speeds depending on how hyped-up they were.

From my twenty-first-century perspective, the Victorian age had been about industrial progress and the growth of the British Empire. What Gwyn remembered it for was militarism and patriotism and the advancement of rights for workers. "It was a time of increasing morality," she told me, and I dutifully wrote that down.

"But it's too obvious to decorate a cake with the Union Jack or create a pie that looks like Queen Victoria's head," said Florence. "I can't be predictable. That's not going to help me tomorrow."

"Steampunk," I suggested, and both Gwyn and Florence stared at me in confusion.

"Steampunk?" Gwyn repeated. "Is that something to do with trains?"

"No. Think of the Gimcrack," I said, and even I understood I was gabbling. That wouldn't help matters. "I mean the look of it—all brass and mechanical stuff." I rubbed my dry eyes. "The judges will understand steampunk. It's a twenty-first-century take on the Victorian age. It emphasises the technological aspects of the era. Kind of... I don't know... H.

169

G. Wells, *Around the World in Eighty Days*, that kind of thing." When both Gwyn and Florence continued to stare at me blankly, I considered giving up. My bed was calling. I sighed and tried one more time. "The way Gorde's Gimcrack looks, with all those cogs and springs and the gold and brass and little ticking things... that's a steampunk kind of look."

"Ah, I see." Florence nodded. "Yes, the technology... the advances in machinery... I could try and capture that. Maybe do a passion fruit sponge—"

"No, no, no!" Gwyn looked positively hurt. "Absolutely not. No."

"No?" Florence asked, her gaze focused on Gwyn.

"We wouldn't have had passion fruit sponge cake back in the day, would we Florence? What's wrong with a good old-fashioned Victoria sponge? What would Mrs Beeton say? I still have all of her books in the attic."

Florence clasped her hands to her mouth in excitement. "Of course. Mrs Beeton! How could I forget? You're a genius, Mrs Daemonne! It makes perfect sense. I'll create authentic Victorian bakes using Mrs Beeton's recipes. That's bound to be a winner! You're a genius!"

I opened my mouth and closed it again. Mrs Daemonne was the genius?

Well, that put Ms Daemonne in her place.

I folded myself against the desk, cheek flat on the paper, and closed my eyes.

Sometimes it was thankless being me.

CHAPTER TWELVE

I arrived downstairs in the kitchen having had only three hours sleep on too much wine. You can imagine what sort of state my head was in. It pounded along to my heartbeat, and my throat was as dry as the Sahara desert. Unfortunately, the kitchen proved to be no refuge. I was met by a scene of total and utter carnage. Monsieur Emietter was shouting at the top of his voice, in French naturally, and while I couldn't understand a word he was saying, I couldn't help noticing he was a little upset.

Several of my kitchen ghosts rushed past me—or through me, which always feels a little unsettling—in their haste to escape the wrath of the rotund chef. I had half a mind to follow them to the nearest exit but quickly remembered the sad and salient fact that, even on a bad head day, Alfhild is in charge.

Pots, pans, dishes and cutlery had been abandoned everywhere. Charity had her hands up and was trying to appease the irate chef in her pidgin French. Quite clearly, he either didn't understand her or was choosing not to listen to her.

"Grandmama?" I called, hoping against hope that she hadn't disappeared without trace again, although I assumed she'd want to see what Florence came up with today in the *Cake Off* tent following the work we'd done so early this morning.

It turned out I'd assumed correctly. Gwyn, perhaps alerted by the sheer volume of fury emanating from the kitchen, apparated in front of me, took stock of the situation and soared across to Monsieur Emietter.

As Charity quickly stepped out of the way, I listened as Gwyn uttered soothing words to the chef. He rapidly fired off a series of curses, gesticulating wildly towards the storerooms. Gwyn, shooting me a frown, spoke once more to the chef, nodding and placating him to the best of her ability. She led him to the kitchen table where he hovered above a bench.

"We'll sort it all out. You really mustn't worry," she told him and nodded at me, even though I had no idea at all just what I was supposed to be sorting.

"We will," I agreed, hastily walking over to join them.

"*Vite! Vite!*" Monsieur Emietter said and placed his head in his hands and sobbed.

"What on earth?" I asked Gwyn.

"Weevils," Gwyn said, her eyes projecting her horror.

"What?" My head thumped like a bass drum. I was never going to drink wine again.

"Weevils?" Charity repeated, standing next to me and looking around in confusion.

"In the flour," Gwyn enlightened us through gritted teeth. "Probably flour beetles rather than weevils actually, but I don't think that makes a great deal of difference to our poor Monsieur Emietter."

I shuddered in response. Insects in the food.

Charity, however, was far quicker on the uptake, mainly because she had gone to bed sober and at a reasonable time. "The flour in the storeroom? The flour that the production crew are going to be requesting in a few hours?"

Gwyn nodded. "Apparently, according to Chef, all of the bags of flour are infested."

"We need to get rid of them!" Charity cried, then looked at me in concern as I gagged. "Are you alright, Alf?"

For one awful moment my stomach tipped over and I thought I might be ill. Insects in the food at

Whittle Inn? This could seriously damage our reputation, of course, but over and above that, it simply made me feel nauseous.

I swallowed hard and shook myself. I needed to get a grasp of the situation. "Ned!" I called, and he appeared lightning fast. "You need to rally the Wonky Inn Ghostly Clean-Up Crew. I want you to remove every trace of flour from the kitchen and storerooms. No exceptions. I want the storerooms swept, hoovered, mopped and rechecked. Got it?"

He nodded and hastened away to grab a few more 'bodies' to assist him with the task. "Charity, I need you to run down to the village and buy every bag of flour, no matter what it is: plain flour, corn-flour, maize flour, rye flour, the works. Buy it all and see if Stan will drive you back here with it. Let's hope there's enough at Whittle Stores to start the bakers off."

"Will do. What are you going to do?"

"I'm going to have a very strong coffee and then I'm going to get on the blower to Rhona to see if her wholesaler can replace our stocks and deliver it all this morning. By the time you get down there, I'll have spoken to her and made the arrangements."

"Okay, boss!" Charity left the kitchen at a run.

"Alfhild," my great-grandmother was saying. "Follow me."

"Can I just grab a coffee first?" I pleaded, but Gwyn glared at me and I dutifully followed her out of the kitchen and down the short corridor to the first storeroom. I pushed it open and we went inside. I was immediately struck by how cool it was.

There were a dozen large sacks of flour neatly lined along the bottom shelves. Flour had been spilt on the floor. This was unusual. We were fastidious about keeping everything neat and tidy in the storerooms. No-one could ever be sure when we might have an inspection from the Food Standards Agency.

I stared at the scene, knowing something was wrong but struggling to process my thoughts.

But then it came to me. The sacks had been ripped open. Every single one. Only one would ever be used at a time. There was no need for the rest to have been opened.

"Did Monsieur Emietter open these?" I asked Gwyn and she shook her head.

"He says not."

I bent down, my thumping headache all but forgotten, and rippled my fingers in the flour. I loved the feel of it, always had, but even as I did so, I could see the beetles. At three or four millimetres long, they were small but hideous in this context.

"This was done on purpose?" I asked in wonder. The room was cool. We would hardly have incubated our own beetles in here, and the fact that all of the sacks had been opened suggested sabotage. No doubt about that.

I stood, and the room spun. I quickly gripped the shelving to steady myself. This was no good. I couldn't think properly when I was dealing with a mild case of self-inflicted blood poisoning.

"I need to make a few phone calls, Grandmama. Can you oversee the removal and proper disposal of this flour and make sure both storerooms are properly cleaned before we have any more delivered?"

"Yes, my dear. Leave it with me." Gwyn nodded approvingly. "Are you going to call your friend at Whittle Stores now?"

"I'm going to start with Millicent," I said. "I need a potion to eradicate this hangover from hell."

Millicent was only too thrilled to head on up to the inn, hoping to catch a glimpse of some of the celebrities working on *The Great Witchy Cake Off.* She brought with her a vial of the most revolting green liquid I had ever seen. It looked like a scraping of toxic plague—or something you might have scooped up from between the rocks in the marsh after the whole of the forest had been sickening for a week. But I knew better than to ask questions. I simply downed the potion in one, much to Millicent's approval, and turned to the more important tasks of the day.

Rhona had been able to re-order all of the flour we would need, and for a small fee, the wholesalers would deliver before ten. As long as Charity had enough to keep the contestants going from nine when the filming began, I figured we might get away with it.

As a courtesy I made a quick phone call to George, who sounded alert and as fresh as a daisy. I filled him in on our potential intruder and he promised to drop by.

I was concerned that someone had been inside the inn, messing with the flour. They'd broken into Rob's van too. Or perhaps, as Silvan had suggested, they had used a djinn. Whoever was behind this, I had to ask myself, did they have something against me and Whittle Inn, or were they trying to sabotage the filming of *The Great Witchy Cake Off?*

I headed upstairs to shower and change, thinking hard all the while. I'd been far too complacent. Silvan had pointed that out—not in so many words—the evening before. My gut feeling was that this series of events—starting with the murder of producer Janice—was not aimed at me personally, but at the series. I tied my hair back in a business-like ponytail, buttoned my robes to the neck and pocketed my wand.

Enough already.

Cake Off fun time was over. I needed to get down to business.

"We're a nation that harks back to the golden era of our grandparents and great-grandparents. To a time when steam trains chuffed through the rolling hills of the countryside, and hot cross buns were one a penny, two a penny. So, what will our five remaining contestants make of Victoriana week? Will they push for the glory of the Empire, or will there be more famine than feast? Stoke up the engine and tighten your stays. It's week four of *The Great Witchy Cake Off*, and it's all to bake for."

"Cut!"

"Was that okay or do you want me to try it again?" Mindi was asking as Jemima and Boo took a quick look back at the recording.

"I think we're good," Boo said, and Jemima agreed. Mindi smiled and relaxed.

"Morning, Alf," a quiet voice greeted me from behind: Bertha, armed as always with a broom. "Everything alright?"

"Yes, thanks." I watched her sweep. "Any reason why it wouldn't be?"

"No, no. I heard you were out late last night, that's all."

"Ha-ha!" I replied. "Yes, I was a little the worse for wear this morning but I'm much better now, thanks to my friend Millicent here."

Bertha and Millicent exchanged pleasantries, Millicent gushing about how much she loved the show, while I peered around at the rest of the production crew, beavering away to make a start on the day's filming. I was relieved to find that the flour that had been kept overnight in the marquee had remained unadulterated. With luck and a following wind, as long as none of the contestants decided to start their bakes over from scratch, we would have more than enough flour to last until the new sacks arrived from the wholesaler.

Bertha finished sweeping and stowed the broom. "We're a little short of cocoa powder and cornflour. And I need to send someone to collect some flour from the stores. Is that alright with you?" Bertha asked.

"Of course!" I said, pretending to be entirely unconcerned, while Millicent, who knew the whole story, cast a suspicious glance at her new friend. "Charity is up at the inn, just give her a shout." Bertha nodded and moved away, and Millicent narrowed her eyes in suspicion.

I shrugged and shook my head. "It's her job," I explained. "She always asks me for permission, and she's the one who organises the supplies to come down from the storeroom."

"So she knows all about the stores and their contents?" Millicent asked in a low hiss.

"Yes, but then so do the runners. She sends one or two of them up to the inn each time."

"I'd keep an eye on her." Millicent folded her arms.

"I don't disagree," I said, keeping my tone mild and stepping well out of the way as one of Bertha's assistants rushed into the marquee with several trays of eggs precariously balanced in one hand and a clipboard in the other.

Millicent raised her eyebrows. "That's a lot of eggs."

"They get through dozens every session," I agreed. "I'm having fresh supplies brought in daily."

"I'm telling you, Alf, you really should get some chickens up here at the inn. You've got bags of room out the back. You'd save a fortune."

"I don't—" I was about to begin protesting again, when the judges entered the marquee.

Millicent's mouth dropped open at the sight of Raoul Scurrysnood and Faery Kerry, making her the oldest fangirl in Devon. She leaned in close to me and whispered, "Can I get Raoul's autograph? Oh, I love him."

Maybe she said it a little louder than she anticipated because he looked over at us and smiled, his glorious eyes lighting up his whole face. Millicent gasped, and I was momentarily concerned she might faint, so I nudged her hard with my elbow.

"Raoul," I said. "This is my friend Millicent. She lives in the village and is one of your biggest fans."

"It's a pleasure to meet you, Millicent." Raoul shook her hand. "You'll have to excuse me though; I need to get started."

"Oh, of course! Carry on, carry on!" Millicent waved him away, blushing bright red. As he joined

Faery Kerry on his mark on the floor, she giggled like a little girl. "Raoul Scurrysnood just spoke to me! I can die happy now."

I laughed. "Well please don't do that just yet."

"Doesn't he make you go weak at the knees, Alf?" Millicent asked, and one of the technicians shot us a quick look. I could see that Millicent was going to be difficult to contain while they were filming.

"Well," I whispered, "I think he's rather sweet, and very handsome, and probably quite charming, but no. He doesn't actually do it for me." I lay my hand on her arm. "Now, Millicent, you need to control yourself because they're going to start rolling in a minute and they need absolute quiet."

"Alright," Millicent chirped playfully. "I'll be good, Alf, I promise. Please don't banish me." She directed this latter to the nearest camera wizard, a young man with long black hair and a nose-ring, who winked at her and set her off again. I pulled her away to the very rear of the marquee, just as the contestants came in.

There were only five of them now. Hortense Briar, Eloise Culpepper, Scampi Porthouse, Davide McGulligan and Florence. We waved at the housekeeper as she passed, like over-excited parents proud of our offspring. I noted how calm she appeared to be in spite of all the furore of the previous evening.

Mindi took her place again, and there was a swift flurry of adjustments to hair and make-up before Bertha asked for silence on the set and Jemima called action. Mindi addressed the camera and recapped on the previous episode before giving her trademark instruction to the contestants: "You're under starter's orders. Recalibrate the scales, flour your pans, turn on your ovens and in three, two, one... Bake!"

Baking pans, glass bowls and utensils clattered loudly as the camera wizards moved into place, zooming in and out as each contestant began their preparation. I watched as Florence carefully shook out flour onto her scales, chopped up butter into small cubes—all without touching anything, of course—and cracked the eggs into what would become her Victorian sponge mixture.

Mindi sidled up to Florence with a camera wizard and a sound witch on her tail. "Welcome back, Florence. Congratulations on making it through to week four."

"Thank you," beamed Florence. "I'm thrilled to have made it this far."

I could have written the script myself. Everyone

said the same things. But maybe that was why we loved it so much.

"So, the theme this week is Victoriana, and you've been asked to produce a cake for this round. Can you tell me what your plan is?" Mindi asked.

"Well—" Florence gestured at the bowl in front of her. "I've decided to keep my cake as traditional as possible. I'm following Mrs Beeton's well-known recipe for a Victoria sponge."

Mindi pretended to look concerned. "Do you think a plain Victoria sponge will be good enough to keep you in the competition, Florence?"

Florence nodded. "I do. Yes. Because it's going to be a good one. I'm sticking to Mrs Beeton's tried and proven recipe. What I have here are equal quantities of butter, sugar and flour. But the trick is, and this is something that many people forget, you also have to have the same weight of egg. You should weigh the eggs in their shells and then make sure you measure out the same amount of butter, sugar and flour. So in my case, my eggs weigh... let me see... 263g, so I need 263g of butter and 263g of flour and sugar." Florence shook the flour into her large mixing bowl. "Trust me, this will be beautifully light and airy and taste like angel's wings."

"Let's hope any angels watching aren't too

distressed by that thought." Mindi turned to the camera and winked. "Are you opting for a traditional strawberry jam filling too, Florence?"

"No. I thought that would be a little too simple. Given that Queen Victoria was the first Empress of India, I felt I could give a nod to India's rich legacy." Florence held up a small bowl. "I've infused some saffron and crushed a palmful of cardamom seeds, so I'm going to add this to the mix instead of milk, with just a little freshly squeezed orange juice. It will taste wonderful!"

"That does sound heavenly. Thanks, Florence!"

"Good, good! Well done, Florence," called Boo. "Keep the cameras rolling please, and can we go to Eloise next, Mindi?"

Florence glanced my way and I gave her the thumbs up.

So far, so good.

Charity popped her head around the door of the tent to give me the heads up that the delivery had arrived and our storeroom had been restocked with new supplies of flour and sugar. I followed her out, away from the sweet scents of baking, into the more autumnal environment of the outside world. My headache had dissipated, and I felt fine, albeit rather hungry. I hadn't had time for breakfast. I could see Rob opening up his van, which reminded me I needed to speak to him about the events of the previous night. Tummy rumbling with desire, I headed his way.

"Morning, Rob," I called as I drew closer.

He looked up from whatever he was doing and nodded. "Morning, Alf."

"Is everything alright with the van?" I asked. "Only I was out here last night with my friend Silvan and he thought you'd had a break-in maybe."

"A break-in?" Rob looked confused and I knew what he was thinking, because the van had been locked up when he'd arrived. "Silvan secured the door for you," I explained.

"Oh right. Well—" Rob looked around. "Every-thing seems to be okay." He opened a few cupboards and looked inside, and then opened his fridge and rummaged around. "Everything is where I would expect it to be."

"And nothing is missing?"

Rob shook his head. "Not as far as I can tell. But what would anyone take from here? All I have is sausages and onions and a huge bag of potatoes in the back of my car."

From behind us came the sound of a klaxon. That signalled the end of the first round.

Torn between the needs of my stomach and my desire to see how Florence had fared in the judging, I reluctantly headed back to the marquee. I waved goodbye to Rob and promised I'd catch him later.

I arrived back into the tent just as Faery Kerry was cutting into Florence's sponge. I was pleased to see how well the cake had risen. It had been sandwiched with a thick layer of cream and a kind of orange marmalade compote. My mouth watered as I watched first Faery Kerry and then Raoul take a forkful of the sponge and chew thoughtfully.

"That's delicious," piped up Faery Kerry. "So moist. The balance of flavours there is exquisite."

Raoul nodded in agreement. "What we have here is a heady mix of skill and creativity. I think you've shown a real flair here, Florence. It tastes delicious. I loved it. Well done!"

Millicent and I exchanged delighted looks. That was the first hurdle accomplished today; the technical challenge was next.

Once all the judging had been completed, there came another break in filming so that everyone could grab a drink and a snack and visit the bathroom, but within twenty minutes the cameras were rolling again.

"This week's technical challenge is a real Victorian favourite, and Faery Kerry, who is old enough to have existed at the time"—Mindi winked cheekily at the camera—"is going to tell you all about it."

"Thank you, Mindi," said Faery Kerry in a voice that mildly castigated the presenter for her joke. "Contestants. This week we're asking you to prepare a Victorian favourite. A staple at many a Victorian tea, and at high tea ever since. Delicacy is the order of the day here. We would like you to prepare thirty-six mini egg custard tarts. We're looking for perfectly crisp cases and sweetly scented middles. You'll have just ninety minutes."

Mindi nodded her thanks. "So, no soggy bottoms, and thirty-six perfect mini egg custard tarts. Got it." Mindi turned back to address the tent as one camera wizard closed in on her face and the other took a panoramic shot of the contestants looking either worried or confident. "You have ninety minutes to produce thirty-six identical egg custard tarts before the judges take a blind taste test. Are you ready? It's time to turn your ovens on once more... and in three, two, one... Bake!"

Florence's egg custard tarts were as exquisite as you would expect. I knew because after the cameras had stopped rolling, the cakes and bakes were sent up to the inn so that everyone could indulge over an extended tea break if they so wished. I guess there must come a time when every person working on *The Great Witchy Cake Off* became heartily sick of sweet goodies.

I hadn't reached that stage quite yet.

"Are they finished for the day?" Charity asked as I walked into the kitchen with Millicent, both of us gagging for a cup of tea.

"They still have to make the showstopper." Millicent sounded extremely knowledgeable about everything *Cake Off* all of a sudden. "It'll be a late one."

"Are you sticking around?" I asked, not really trying to get rid of her, just because I already knew the answer.

"What leave now and miss the chance of setting eyes on the sultry Mr Scurrysnood again? Are you kidding?"

"He's far too young for you." I shook my head.

Charity snorted. "Age is a state of mind. Don't listen to her, Mills."

"I may take up permanent residence here," Millicent replied archly. "Do you have a room going spare? I don't want to miss any of the delicious Mr Scurrysnood's comings and goings. And anyway, did you see the way he looked at me? He appreciates a woman with a full figure and soft edges."

"There's hope for us all." I smirked.

"Well, thank heavens for that," Charity said. "I'd begun to despair of ever finding anyone decent."

"It's a small pool to fish from here in Whittlecombe," I admitted. "Mind you, there's always Alex Bramble."

"It didn't go well last night then?" asked Charity. "You're giving up on him already?"

"I don't think I spoke five sentences to him all night. No, he's not for me." I remembered Silvan saying exactly that.

Hmpf. What did Silvan know?

"Shame. By the way, Alf, you have a visitor upstairs."

Good news.

"Already? Smashing. I'll head on up there." Then, nodding at Millicent, I said to Charity, "Keep Miss Whittlecombe 1978 here out of trouble, will you?"

"Roger that," Charity said, and we both laughed.

Millicent pretended to mince her way along a catwalk as Monsieur Emietter looked on in bewilderment.

"Hey, Ross." I raised my eyebrows at the ghost sitting at my computer, furiously tapping away on the keyboard. "Good to see you again."

"It's lovely to be back." He looked up momentarily, offered a half-smile, and then went back to what he was doing.

"Is there something wrong with my machine?" I asked in alarm.

"Just updating your virus protection and cleaning some files."

"Wouldn't you have needed my password or fingerprint?"

Ross favoured me with his most scathing look. "Please," he said.

"Sorry." I hovered beside him feeling suitably chastised, waiting to speak again until he'd finished.

Finally, he sat back. "All done."

"How has it been? Working with Penelope Quigwell?" I asked, hoping he'd be able to dish some dirt on the peculiar woman who managed most of

Whittle Inn's legal and financial affairs and assisted Wizard Shadowmender with similar issues and challenges. She led a team of computing and technical wizards who had used their magick skills to good effect recently in order to untangle The Mori's financial affairs and help us defeat them.

"Great. Really interesting," Ross said.

"Oh, right." Not the answer I'd been hoping for. Not very exciting at all.

"There's always something juicy to get into." Ross smiled properly, something he rarely did. "You know what? Dying and meeting you, Alf, I think those were the best things that could have happened to me."

That's called putting a positive spin on things. "I'm glad," I replied, and I kind of was, but still thought living your actual life before death was preferable.

"So, what can I do for you?" Ross got down to business.

I opened the desk drawer next to him and pulled out Raoul's phone, wrapped in its plastic evidence bag. George had entrusted it to me for the time being.

"There was a murder here in the grounds of the inn a few days ago. A witch by the name of Janice

Tork-Mimosa was stabbed. She was a producer at Witchflix, so quite important. This phone belongs to Raoul Scurrysnood." I placed it gently on the top of my desk and looked expectantly at Ross, but he showed no recognition at either name. Perhaps he hadn't been dead long enough, or maybe he just didn't have time to watch television.

"You remember George? DS George Gilchrist?" I asked, and this time Ross nodded. "He's investigating the murder, but obviously there's a crossover between the mortal and magickal worlds and I want to help him out."

"Alright."

"Raoul had been having a relationship with Janice, but he broke it off after he received some emails suggesting she was having an affair with Pierre de Corduroy." When Ross again looked blank, I filled in the gap. "Pierre is a hotshot fashion designer. His designs are always on the front of *Witch in Vogue*."

"Sounds pretty sordid all round," remarked Ross.

"Indeed." I couldn't disagree. These were the lives our witchy celebrities seemed to enjoy living. "However, the emails and the video links Raoul claimed he received can't be found by normal police methods, which is why we decided to turn to you."

"Fun," Ross said, and his hands hovered over the phone. The screen lit up and Ross began scrolling, simply using his own thoughts. Faster and faster the screens changed as Ross looked through the most obvious apps. "So, you want me to see if I can find any traces of these emails to Raoul, and who sent them?"

"If you could, that would be perfect."

"I'll certainly give it a go." Ross peered up at me. "There *is* something else to consider of course."

"What's that?"

"The messages were never there in the first place and your Raoul is simply covering his tracks."

He certainly had a point. The thought hadn't even crossed my mind. I'd bought into the judge's story hook, line and sinker. Ross had obviously been hanging around Penelope for longer than was good for him.

"Either way you'll be able to tell that, right?"

Ross bent over the phone once more, the screens just a blur. "Oh, I should think so," he said, and I swear I'd never heard him sound more cheerful.

Zephaniah and Charity were busy cleaning up the dining area when I headed back downstairs. I quickly grabbed a plate and stole some of the remaining bakes. Florence's egg custard mini tartlets were long gone, so I had to make do with someone else's—impossible to tell whose, but I knew they weren't Florence's—and they really didn't make the grade. Florence's splendid ' orange, saffron and cardamom infused Victoria sponge had also been demolished, so I settled for a slice of strawberry sponge instead. I have to admit, grudgingly, that it at least tasted pretty decent.

The production crew and contestants had disappeared, and the only tea on offer had long since stewed, so I decided to grab a blackcurrant and soda from behind the bar. Ned was there, polishing glasses and restocking the fridges.

Standing at the pump, dispensing soda into a pint glass, I distinctly heard Ned say, *"Mine eye hath play'd the painter and hath stell'd, thy beauty's form in table of my heart; my body is the frame wherein 'tis held—"*

I looked sideways at him and he stopped and ducked his head.

"That was pretty," I said, trying to encourage him, but he only looked sheepish. "Was that poetry?"

"Shakespeare, Miss Alf."

"Well, it was lovely." I tipped blackcurrant cordial into my glass and added an extra measure because I liked to be able to taste it. "Is it for someone special?" I asked.

Ned looked scandalised. "No!"

"Oh. Okay. As you were." I backed away, pretending to be engaged with cleaning the drops dripping from the bottom of the glass.

"*My body is the frame wherein 'tis held, and perspective it is the painter's art,*" Ned continued, stumbling over a few of the words.

Curious. It looked like my odd-job man-of-all-trades was learning poetry.

Bless him.

Poetry and dancing?

Who on earth was he trying to impress?

"I'm behind with the bedrooms," Charity announced when I carried my empties through to the kitchen. I regarded her guiltily. With Florence in the *Cake Off* tent and me flitting in and out so I could watch the filming, the burden of the housekeeping was falling on poor Charity.

"I'm sorry," I said sheepishly. "I'll help you out before I go and see how Florence is getting on."

I climbed the stairs and poked my head into the office to see how Ross was doing. He had Raoul's phone hooked up to his own chunky laptop and was scowling in concentration at whatever data was showing on the screen. I backed out of the room without disturbing him.

I have five rooms on this floor, and I didn't expect the housekeeping to take long. For the most part, it didn't. Bertha the floor manager was as neat and tidy as I'd expected, and Faery Kerry's room was immaculate. So immaculate, in fact, it led me to believe she had waved her magick wand and cleaned it herself before she started work in the *Cake Off* tent that morning. I emptied the bins, straightened the already made bed and dusted around. Job done.

Raoul's room was a similar story, except the bed was unmade, while Mindi's room had the faint stench of stale cigarette smoke. I squirted the air with Florence's favourite room freshening spray. The scent of raspberries and rhubarb flavoured the air. Much better.

The final room on the corridor had briefly belonged to Janice Tork-Mimosa. George had taken her meagre belongings to the station on the day she'd been murdered, and so I had allocated the room to her replacement, Murgatroyde Snippe.

"By all that's green!"

I stood in the doorway and surveyed the wreckage of Murgatroyde's room, wondering if I'd make it back to see Florence finish her showstopper. Where the other rooms had been reasonable, Murgatroyde was one of those guests who could bring a housekeeper to tears. There were clothes all over the floor, strewn about with total abandon. Numerous glasses and cups had been dumped on every surface, and make-up littered the dressing table. Given that the room would have been cleaned just twenty-four hours previously, it seemed incredible to me that she had managed to make so much mess in so short a time.

Sighing, I set to work, moving quickly and efficiently through each task, starting higher up, as I'd been taught—cleaning surfaces and so on—then making the bed and finally clearing up the floor so I could hoover.

Murgatroyde's suitcase lay half under the bed, so I pulled it out. It was one of those soft cases that closed with a three-quarter length zip. It was open, so I tried to zip it up to stop the dust from getting inside. When the zip stuck, I pulled it back and had another go. Something inside the case was catching. I unzipped the whole thing and peered inside the case. A black and white scarf in soft merino wool lay on top of a couple of pairs of shoes, its end snagged in the zip. I gently eased it free, folded it neatly and tucked it away before zipping up the case and stowing it beneath the bed.

The bathroom looked like an artist had tripped over with a pallet full of paints in their hand. More concealer, blusher and eyeshadow stained the sink and even the bath. There was nothing for it. I gritted my teeth and got down to business, scrubbing at each and every surface, spraying and wiping, until the bathroom gleamed.

"As shiny as a new sixpence." Gwyn's voice startled me.

"Were sixpences particularly shiny?" I asked.

"Only when they were new," Gwyn replied. "Having fun, dear?"

"I'm just about finished. Charity is going to hoover and mop."

"How is young Florence getting on?" Gwyn asked, arching one of her perfect eyebrows.

"I think she was in or around first place after the technical. I'm going to go down and see how the showstopper bake is going now. Why don't you come with me?"

"I'll see you down there," Gwyn said, and the air shimmered as she disappeared. I collected up my cleaning materials, and with one more quick look around the bedroom, satisfied that the room was clean and tidy, I let myself out and headed down the stairs.

Florence's showstopper was a triumph. She'd elected to create a model of the Crystal Palace, where The Great Exhibition had been held in 1851. She'd plumped for a white strawberry sponge cake with hints of basil, and a more intense flavoured strawberry filling. The cake had been covered in white chocolate frosting and then decorated with basil-flavoured sugar glass windows, with darker chocolate outlines where needed. Florence had piped a green fondant base onto a cake stand and then made a dozen or so tiny Victorian figures—the women in crinolines and the men in top hats—who appeared to be walking around the building itself.

"Darn it, that's cute," I muttered to Millicent as the judges cut into the structure.

"It's impressive for sure," Millicent nodded, but her tone suggested mild disapproval, and I wondered if this champion of the uber-traditional Whittlecombe WI considered it a little over the top. She would never have said so.

"It is a baking competition," I reminded her, just in case she'd forgotten.

Poor old Hortense suffered a complete disaster. Not only did her cake have a soggy bottom, but an entire layer also appeared to have imploded. She'd been trying to recreate Victoria's coronation crown and sceptre, but the icing had run and the whole thing looked like somebody had mistaken it for a cushion and sat on it. Hortense's eyes filled with tears, and the other contestants consoled her as best they could.

Mindi took her place and the cameras rolled around. One kept a focus on the presenter and the other took close-ups of Florence, Scampi, Hortense, Eloise and Davide.

"It's been a day of drama for you all. So without further ado, I'm going to reveal this week's star baker. The contestant who will be crowned Empress of the bakes after the Victorian challenge, is—"

There was a long silence, all the better to ramp up the sense of expectation in the room.

"Florence!" Mindi announced, and there was a rippling of applause. I had to clamp my hands to my mouth to stop myself from shouting out in glee. Florence looked stunned and then jigged on the spot as the other contestants congratulated her.

"And now I have the sad task of announcing the name of the contestant who will be leaving us today. The person being banished to the workhouse, is—"

Again, a lengthy pause and I found myself clenching my fists in agitation even though I knew Florence was already through to the next day.

"Hortense." A collective 'aah' filled the tent, the sound of multiple people expressing their regret. We all joined in, everyone lamenting the loss of one more person even though the whole idea was that the last one standing in the competition was the winner and if we didn't get rid of somebody then nobody would win.

"Sorry, Hortense," said Mindi, and enveloped her in a hug. The contestants grouped together and the judges quickly moved to join them, Raoul shaking hands with Hortense and Faery Kerry giving her a quick cuddle before engaging Florence in discussion about her clever use of sugar glass.

"And cut!" shouted Jemima.

"That's a wrap." Boo leaned back on his seat and stretched.

Bertha ran forward to move the cakes to a trolley to be taken up to the inn, while her team began to clear the contestants' kitchens of all the remaining ingredients. My own Wonky Inn Ghostly Clean-Up Crew arrived to undertake the deep cleaning required after the day's filming.

I watched everyone work, aware that any of them could have contaminated the flour sacks when clearing up the previous evening. At this time of day, Monsieur Emietter would have already produced his evening meal and it was unlikely that he would need to go into the storerooms again. He wouldn't have noticed any issue with the flour until he arrived in the morning.

The contamination had almost certainly come from someone engaged in the production, and it seemed logical to imagine that, by extension, they might be the person responsible for Janice's murder. I found it unlikely that either of the judges, or Mindi, would have an excuse to go into the kitchen. So didn't that leave the production crew?

I watched them all working and found myself wishing I knew more about them.

CHAPTER THIRTEEN

"Morning, Ross." I slipped into my office before breakfast to sort out a few things. *The Great Witchy Cake Off* crew would only be here for another few days, then the inn would be getting back to normal and I'd have a whole load of new (and old) guests returning. Halloween was just a matter of weeks away after all, and I liked the idea of celebrating Samhain with a full heart this year.

And without vampires.

Ross, who of course did not need sleep, was staring at the screen on his laptop. I peered over his shoulder, but all I could see were blocks of rapidly changing numbers, entirely meaningless to me. "How's it going?"

Ross frowned. "I have to say this is one unexpectedly tough challenge. So far I've been able to establish that magick *has* been used to eliminate some messages that were sent to Raoul's phone, but I can't find where that magick originated, or who was responsible for it or what the messages were." A few buttons clicked on the keyboard beneath his translucent fingers. The numbers slowed down temporarily and then with another series of clicks, sped up again. "I've been in touch with the office." He presumably meant where he worked with Penelope Quigwell and the other technical wizards. "But don't worry. I'm intrigued now. We will get to the bottom of it one way or another." He sat back and huffed.

"Oh I know you will," I replied with more confidence than I felt. "Erm..." I needed to ask for another favour. Or two. "Listen, there's something else."

"Oh yes?"

"This needs to be entirely hush-hush." I lowered my voice and leaned towards him, winking conspiratorially.

"I'm good at hush-hush. I'm a ghost now. We don't make a lot of noise."

I studied Ross's deadpan face, wondering whether this was his idea of making a joke. "Ha. Ah... Would you be able to track down some information on a member of the production crew? Her name is Bertha Crumb."

"Date of birth?"

I shook my head. "I have no idea. She's approximately twenty-four or so, I'd say. Lives in London usually."

"Not a huge amount of help. What kind of thing are you looking for?"

"She works for Witchflix, on *The Great Witchy Cake Off*. Surely you can cross-reference her from that? Her employment records or something? I just want to know who she is, what she's done in the past, anything slightly suspicious. Links to Janice Tork-Mimosa, that kind of thing."

Ross nodded. "That seems simple enough."

"I appreciate it."

I made a move towards the door. "There was one other thing."

"Okay?" Ross raised his eyebrows and I could tell he was amused.

"It's probably something and nothing. It's just I have an odd sensation about somebody, and I've learned of late that it's probably best to listen to these feelings."

Ross nodded. "I think I've been hanging around enough witches to understand what you're saying." He snorted softly. "Now there's a sentence I never had a chance to say when I was alive."

"His name is Crispin Cavendish. He's—"

"A relative of Lyle?" Of course Ross knew who Lyle was.

"His brother apparently."

"Do you think he's something to do with The Mori?"

I shrugged. "I really don't know. We never fully understood how deeply Lyle was involved, did we?"

"The investigations into him are ongoing." Ross's tone was mild, but I sensed a hint of steel there too. The Mori were an organisation Wizard Shadow-mender and Penelope Quigwell were intent on elim-inating forever.

"It's not Crispin's involvement or non-involve-ment with The Mori that bothers me. Although obvi-ously if he is involved, that would be good to know too."

"Well what then?"

I laughed. "It probably sounds silly. It's a little personal. Millicent and I have a friend in the village named Sally McNab-Martin. She's recently taken up with this Crispin and I just don't trust him. I want to protect Sally."

"Ah, I see." Ross scratched his head. "Affairs of the heart seem so important to those who still live, don't they?"

"Just to humans? Don't ghosts continue

searching for a soulmate too?" I was thinking of Ned, of course.

"Hmm." Ross gave that some thought. "I don't know. You'd have to choose wisely, wouldn't you? Eternity is a long time to be with the wrong person."

"There is that, I suppose." I smiled at Ross's pessimism. I guessed if he'd been more upbeat about life in general, he would never have thrown himself in front of a train in the first place.

"I'll look into it." Ross leaned over his laptop once more. I could see our conversation was over.

"Thanks. Let me know if you find anything," I said. When he didn't reply, I closed the door quietly and left him to it.

Millicent was waiting for me in the kitchen when I went down. "Are you here again?" I asked.

"I can't keep away from your scintillating and sparkling personality, that's what it is, Alf."

I grinned, knowing full well that she just wanted to spend more time in Raoul's company. "Well seeing as you're here, maybe you could help me out with breakfast," I said, and set her to tea and coffee dispensing duties while I carried through endless plates of toast.

"What's the theme for *Cake Off* today?" Millicent asked while we wiped down tables afterwards.

"The Natural World," Charity called out from behind the bar. She was loading the glasswasher with juice glasses.

"I can't see Florence having any trouble with that," I said.

"It's the final tomorrow. I really hope she goes through." Millicent echoed what we were all thinking.

"Then it's back to normal," Charity said, pushing the button on the washer. A whoosh of water confirmed it was working. She came out from behind the bar, wiping her hands on a towel. "It'll be a relief, although at the same time it's always a shame to say goodbye to some of these guests."

"Maybe they'll come back again," Millicent suggested.

I wasn't entirely sure I wanted them back. Not until we'd worked out who had killed Janice and who had contaminated the flour. But I held my tongue and hoped against hope that upstairs, Ross's diligent fingers were unearthing something that would help us.

The filming had already begun when I crept into the marquee a little later. Millicent had taken up her position, her keen eyes observing Raoul as he moved among the four remaining contestants to quiz them about their bakes. As always, the bakers had started with the signature challenge. Today's task was to create a loaf of bread in the shape of a hedgehog.

Florence's breadmaking skills were second to none. I was more than confident she'd be able to pull this off without any trouble. I noticed that Scampi had started his dough again, however, and given how little time there was left, I couldn't see how he would manage to prove the loaf and bake it before Mindi counted down to the end of the task.

"What's going to lift your loaf above the others, Florence?" Faery Kerry was asking my housekeeper, and Florence smiled knowingly.

"I'm using a marmalade glaze," she said. "It will give the hedgehog a great colour on top."

"And what about the prickles?" The contestants were forbidden from sticking anything in the finished loaf.

"It's all about perception," Florence explained and looked straight at the camera. "See here—" She bent over the loaf and directed the camera wizard to follow where she was pointing. "I've created quite deep cuts in the dough. Obviously in the final prove, and once the loaf starts to bake, it will lose some of that definition, but not all of it. With the help of the glaze"—Florence made her little bowl of marmalade jam hover in front of the camera—"you'll get a sense of dark and light, shadow and depth." With a wiggle of her finger, the pastry brush whipped into the deep crevices she had cut on the back of her shaped loaf. "It will be quite obvious that this little munchkin is a spiky hedgehog." The brush returned to the bowl and was set down gently on the counter. Florence smiled at the camera.

"Excellent work, Florence," said Boo. "You're a natural. Camera—keep rolling. Faery Kerry? Let's move on to Scampi."

"Well, well," Millicent whispered to me. "Who'd have thought our shy and retiring ghost would be a TV star?"

"I'm not sure she's ever been shy and retiring," I said. "Although she's certainly always been an astounding baker."

"I taught her that trick with the marmalade, you know?" Millicent said, just loud enough that Raoul, who had walked off set for a short break, could hear.

He smiled at Millicent while I regarded my older witch friend with healthy scepticism, unsure whether she was telling porky pies or not.

Florence's loaf was every bit as good as she had described. Scampi's loaf was, as expected, a complete disaster. It hadn't been proved enough and hadn't baked enough either. Eloise's loaf was better, but too salty. That left Florence and Davide. Given that Davide's loaf didn't look like a hedgehog at all—more like roadkill in fact—Florence won the round hands down.

The technical challenge was to prepare twenty-four shortbread biscuits, shaped as flowers. I observed as Florence happily jumped in, measuring flour and sugar and butter, and then mixing icing sugar together with flavourings. She produced two dozen magnificently delicate rose and rhubarb flavoured biscuits, beautifully iced in three shades of pink. The deeper, almost reddy-pink icing added depth to the look, and tiny transparent sugar glass balls decorated the middle of each biscuit, looking for all the world like drops of dew on soft petals.

"Job done, I think." I nudged Millicent. "How can she fail to go through after that?"

I didn't have a chance to find out. As the judges bent to taste a section of one of Florence's gorgeous creations, Charity burst into the marquee and grabbed my arm to drag me outside.

"What's up?" I asked as soon as we were clear of the tent.

"No gas."

"No gas?" I repeated. What did she mean?

"There's no gas coming into the inn. Monsieur Emietter can't cook. The central heating isn't working either. The hot water's alright because we have the back boiler."

"Have you phoned the gas company?"

Of course she had. Charity was more than capable. "They said there's nothing their end, so it must be an issue at the inn. They're sending a team out. They'll be here within the hour."

That was quick, but probably not quick enough to salvage Monsieur Emietter's dinner plans. A sudden burst of laughter to our left caught my attention. On the edge of the gardens, Rob was hanging over the counter sharing a joke with one of the make-up artists.

"All is not lost," I said. "I have a cunning plan. Looks like it's sausage and mash all round tonight."

I spent most of the afternoon dashing between the inn and the marquee. On the one hand I wanted to keep an eye on Florence's progress, and on the other I wanted to get to the bottom of the gas supply problem. Our gas company turned up and ran some checks but couldn't find anything wrong with any of our appliances. However, the gas wasn't getting into the inn. Somewhere there had to be a leak. By process of elimination, the workers eventually found it at the bottom of the lane, where my land met the edge of Whittlecombe.

Fortunately, the ovens in the *Cake Off* tent were unaffected as they were running from the electric, but that was hardly going to pacify an irate Monsieur Emietter.

When I enquired about the length of time it would take to fix the problem, I was met with that familiar tradesmen's trait of sucking in air while raising eyebrows. I impressed upon the gas workers the urgency of having gas at the inn—both for heating and cooking purposes—and they said they would get onto it straight away.

I didn't hold out much hope, but that was the state of play.

Next, I had to check with Rob that he would be able to cater for more of the production crew than he might normally. He happily confirmed he could, and I thought about offering him one of my ghosts to help chop onions etc., but seeing as Rob didn't really know about the ghosts of Whittle Inn, I decided that might take too much explaining and in any case lead to some difficult questions. However, I did promise that either Charity or myself would come and help him serve after filming had finished for the day.

It was the least I could do.

As I finished with Rob, I turned back towards the inn and spotted Silvan lounging on a stripy deckchair in front of the main steps. It made for an incongruous sight and I stood for a moment and regarded him with suspicion. He might have been watching the goings-on in the grounds, but his hat was pulled down over his face and he appeared to all intents and purposes to be sleeping.

I knew him better than that though.

I headed that way, and when I was close enough, kicked the bottom of his boot.

"Good afternoon, Alfhild," he drawled without so much as peeping at me. As I'd anticipated, he knew exactly what was going on everywhere. "You seem to be frightfully busy this afternoon. It's a wonder you don't have raised blood pressure."

"My blood pressure is fine, thank you. Nothing I can't handle."

"Oh, I don't doubt it." He lazily pulled his hat away from his face and smiled his laconic smile. "What's going on?"

"Absolutely nothing you need to worry about."

He yawned and stretched. "That's good. I wasn't in the mood for fighting any battles this afternoon."

"There are no battles to be fought here." I looked at him, so totally relaxed, his feet splayed out in front of him. "What are *you* up to though? It's not exactly warm enough to be sunbathing."

Silvan pointed up at the sky. "See that big yellow thing? That's the sun. If I lie underneath it, that's sunbathing surely? It doesn't matter how warm it is. Apparently the Vitamin D it gives off is good for you no matter what time of year it is."

"I wouldn't know," I said. Even on holiday in the summer I would keep covered up. If I absolutely had to go out during the day, I'd lathered myself in Witch Factor 500. "I'm not really a fan of extreme weather."

"Being pale suits you, Alfhild, but the sun brings your freckles out, and by all that's green, that's pretty cute."

His amused laugh floated across the gardens and

I lay my hand on his shoulder. "Shush," I growled at him. "They're filming. They don't like a lot of noise outside."

"I'm sure they can't hear me."

I shook my head at him in exasperation and moved away. I'd leave him to his own amusement.

"Are you going inside?" he called after me, "Only I'd love a drink."

"What did your last slave die of?" I muttered, not gracing him with a response, but after quickly discussing the evening's dinner arrangements with Charity, I made my way into the kitchen. Gwyn had a large copper of boiling water on the go, so I made a pot of tea and returned to Silvan with a large mug.

"I was thinking more of a glass of whisky, to be honest," he replied in lieu of thanks.

I held my hand out to take the mug back from him and sighed. "Give me the tea," I said. "I'll have it if you don't want it. You know where the bar is, after all. Or if you're feeling *that* lazy, just give Zephaniah or Ned a shout."

"Old Ned has bigger fish to fry, I think." Silvan's eyes glinted in amusement.

"What do you know?" I asked. How could Silvan know more about what was going on with Ned than I did?

Silvan merely laughed. "I couldn't possibly betray a confidence."

A confidence? Had Ned seriously taken Silvan into his confidence? Why not me? Weren't we friends? I pouted. When I tried to take the mug of tea away from Silvan, he waved me away.

"No, it's mine now. You made it for me, and I would never look such a gift horse in the mouth."

"Oh, fine," I huffed. "I'm going back down to the marquee to see how Florence is getting on. When you've finished 'sunbathing' or whatever it is you're doing out here, if you could return the mug to the kitchen, I would be most grateful."

"I'm a guest here, don't you know?" Silvan reminded me. "You're actually supposed to be waiting on me hand and foot."

"Hell will freeze over before that happens," I retorted, ignoring the mirth I saw in his eyes. "Which reminds me, I can't serve you dinner tonight either because there won't be any. You'll need to go into Whittlecombe I'm afraid."

"Ah yes, your little gas problem." So he *did* know. Nothing escaped Silvan.

"Exactly. Sorry to inconvenience you," I told him, and then quickly walked away. He slunk back down into his deckchair and replaced his hat over his eyes, but for some reason I could still feel those eyes burning into the back of my head as I went.

Florence had called her showstopper 'Forest Fayre'.

"Ingenious," announced Raoul.

"Incredibly pretty," trilled Faery Kerry.

The camera wizard slowly panned around the cake and then fell back, allowing me a chance to get a better look. Mindi began the voiceover. "Florence has crafted a tree stump from a chocolate cake with caramel crème and a chocolate mocha flavoured glaze. She's covered the stump in tiny marzipan flowers and three dozen tiny creatures. Twelve chocolate orange flavoured squirrels with an orange and Cointreau flavoured icing, twelve vanilla flavoured badgers with a slight aniseed flavoured icing, and twelve carrot cake foxes with toffee-apple flavoured icing. In addition, we see more of her now infamous sugar work taking the form of butterflies and ladybirds."

"Keep rolling," Boo called out from behind his digital display. "We'll do that again in the editing, Mindi. It's fine for now."

"You're sure?" Mindi asked.

"Yes, yes," Boo said. "Okay judges. Are we ready?"

Superlatives filled the tent as Faery Kerry and Raoul Scurrysnood, both notoriously honest in their judging, lent their taste buds to the critiquing process. Every nibble seemed to heap ever more praise on my housekeeper, and I realised with a start that this programme was set to make Florence a baking superstar. Even if she didn't win the competition outright, nobody who tuned in to this episode would ever forget her Forest Fayre and the teeny animals that lived on a fallen tree trunk.

I sniffed and dashed away a tear.

"Are you crying?" Millicent, standing beside me, asked.

"Oh shush," I said. "I've got something in my eye." But really, my heart had swollen with pride. My Florence, performing so magnificently. She had moved me to tears with her gracious brilliance.

Millicent and I waited with bated breath, but there was no reason to worry. For the second day running, Florence was named star baker, and this time it was Davide who was heading home.

The cameras finally stopped rolling for the day and we all began milling around the tent offering congratulations and commiserations where appropriate. Bertha and her crew began the clearing up, and the cakes were transported to the inn, which reminded me about dinner.

"Oh hey, guys!" I shouted above the general din. "Hey, everyone?".

When I finally managed to get their attention, I explained the situation. "The gas company have located the leak but they won't finish the repairs until tomorrow—so for tonight, I'd like to invite you to try out Rob Parker's Porky Perfection if you haven't already. In the morning, if we can't manage a cooked breakfast for you, Rob will open early with sausage, bacon or egg baps."

"Or any combo of those," suggested Millicent, and there were murmurs of approval.

Only Patty Cake turned her nose up at the news. "Well, I'll eat at The Hay Loft," she said with a sniff. "Would anyone care to join me?"

Raoul shrugged, easy-going, and probably not particularly hungry after a day of eating cake. I thought Murgatroyde might, because she opened her mouth to say something in reply. Her mobile phone picked that moment to erupt into a cheery electronic tune, so she hooked it out of her pocket to answer it instead.

"Snippe," she said casually, but when she heard

who was on the other end, her demeanour changed. She straightened up, and I couldn't help but notice as her face suddenly clouded. "I see. But—" She listened a little more. "I understand that, but we film the final tomorrow." One hand crept to her mouth, then fell away again. "Sir. Yes. The thing is—"

Sir? Who could she be talking to? That single word seemed to put Patty on edge too, and even Raoul, normally so laid back, glanced over and frowned in concern.

"Alright. I'll tell them." Murgatroyde's voice weakened. "Yes. Thank you, sir. Bye."

She thumbed the screen and the call ended, then turned to face the rest of us. "I have some bad news," she said. "That was our bosses from Witchflix. They've seen the rough cut of the first few shows we shot earlier this week."

"Well what's wrong with them?" Patty asked, peering closely at her co-producer from behind her dark glasses. "I supervised the editing myself. There was nothing untoward, surely?"

Murgatroyde shook her head. "They say we've broken the rules of *The Great Witchy Cake Off.*"

Patty screwed her face up in consternation. "Broken the rules? That's preposterous. We've done everything the way we normally would, haven't we? What's changed?"

Murgatroyde pointed at Florence. "The contestants. The way we've chosen them. Florence isn't a witch. And the big bosses have stated that *only* witches can participate in *The Great Witchy Cake Off*."

Florence's mouth dropped open in sudden horror at what she knew was coming, and I rocked back on my heels in dismay.

"So what do they want us to do? We only have the final to film, and we're doing that tomorrow." Patty's voice rose in panic.

Murgatroyde's mouth turned down at the corners. "We have to disqualify Florence." She turned to my housekeeper with a grimace. "Sorry, Florence, you're out."

CHAPTER FOURTEEN

I sat on a bench in the clearing of Speckled Wood, absently stroking Mr Hoo's head, hardly hearing him when he twitted at me. Eventually, when I didn't respond to him, he gave me a swift nip on the finger with his sharp little beak.

"Oi!" I cried. "Do you mind?"

"Hoo-oooo. Hoooooo."

"I wasn't ignoring you, I was just otherwise engaged," I protested, sucking on my finger. He hadn't broken the skin so my only injury would be a little bruise there.

"Hoooooooo. Hoo hoo."

"I don't want to go and see Vance. I don't think he can help me," I said. "I don't think anyone can. I just feel sad for Florence. She's worked so hard and she's come so far… it seems harsh to take the chance of participating in the final away from her. She deserved more than that."

Mr Hoo hoo'd sadly. "Hoo."

"Yes. I'm sad too."

"Hoo ooh. Hoo!"

I smiled down at my cheeky little friend. "Listen, Mr Feathery Clever Clogs. You're probably right. I *haven't* been getting enough sleep and I *am* fretting about a variety of things. Too many things." I stared out into the dark shadows of the forest around me. "For starters, I wish I knew who was behind the death of Janice. I suppose we should be thankful for small mercies that nobody else has been killed this week. It's not like we have a serial murderer on our hands."

"Hoo!" Mr Hoo sounded shocked.

"I'm not being complacent at all. I'm just saying it could be worse." Plus, maybe I felt a slight disconnect from it all because the threat had been aimed at one individual whom I didn't know very well, and not at me or the inn.

"Although that's a pretty rubbish way to think of it," I scolded myself. "At the end of the day the poor woman was on my property at the time of her demise, and surely that means I'm culpable in some way."

I leaned forward and put my head in my hands.

"Hooo oooh," Mr Hoo called sadly.

"Why are you saying that? I'm not lonely," I insisted. "I have lots of friends." I blinked away the tears that had started to form. "Charity, Millicent. George, kind of." My voice trailed away to virtually nothing. "I have you and the ghosts and Grandmama and Vance."

Pretend friends? asked a niggly voice in my head.

They are *not* pretend friends, I insisted to myself. As if to prove just that, I jumped to my feet and made my way along the path, heading for the marsh after all, but before I could arrive at Vance's pool, I heard the now familiar sound of an Elizabethan madrigal. Luppitt was out here, and that could only mean one thing.

Ned was dancing.

I crept forward, inch by quiet inch, peering through the foliage until I could make out the slightly shiny persona of my jack-of-all-trades. He'd obviously been putting in a great deal of practice because whereas before his movements had appeared stilted and slightly off-kilter, now they were more confident and had a certain grace to them. I watched until he'd finished and silently applauded.

"Oh bravo, bravo!" Vance boomed, and from the cacophony that followed, I could only imagine he was shaking his branches. Twigs and old birds' nests, insects and all manner of detritus rained down around me. I covered my hair with my hands and crouched low to the ground. "You could make a living on the stage, young Neddy!"

Luppitt laughed and agreed. "Hark! You should join the Devonshire Fellows, Ned. We'll make our fortunes yet, forsooth!"

I listened to them having fun and backed slowly away. I was dying with curiosity to find out more about Ned and the object of his affections, but for now, I just let them enjoy the forest by themselves.

Silvan had often told me I was nosy. Well, tonight I was minding my own business.

Except I quickly changed my mind when I arrived home at the inn. Before heading for my bedroom, I popped my head around the office door to check on Ross. This time he cheerfully waved me inside.

"I have something for you," he announced, looking mightily pleased with himself.

"The videos?" I asked hopefully. They would help us eliminate Raoul, and I have to admit that Millicent's hero worshipping of the green-eyed baking god seemed to be rubbing off on me. I liked him. I sincerely hoped he was not the murderer of Janice Tork-Mimosa.

"No. Sorry to disappoint you. I *am* making some headway on those, but I'm waiting for some triangulation on co-ordinates, and that means working with my head office, as you know."

I did know.

"They won't be rushed," Ross said firmly.

"But the production crew finish filming tomorrow and then they'll disperse. I'm worried George—DS Gilchrist—won't get the arrest he wants for this case."

Ross shrugged. Such things made no difference to him; he was a data man through and through.

"So, what do you have then?"

"Crispin Cavendish."

Well, that was something! "Spill the beans, Ross," I said impatiently.

Ross waved a finger and a printout floated through the air and into my hand. It contained facts pertinent to Lyle's brother. His full name and address. Date of birth and... I did a double take. "He's married?"

"He certainly is," said Ross, returning to his screen. "With two children."

"Separated then?"

"I don't think so." Ross shook his head, and absently directed another piece of paper my way. I studied the printout in disbelief. Crispin had—that very morning—booked a holiday for himself, his wife and their two children to Australia for Christmas, still over ten weeks away. Not the act of a man who was estranged from his wife.

"What a rat!" I spat and began ruminating on how I could stitch him up.

Sometime in the early hours of the morning I found myself suddenly blinking into the darkness, unsure what had awoken me.

It could have been the fact that Crispin was a liar and a cheat... and we all know how much I hate those.

Ribbit.

Or it might have been the sense of injustice I felt for Florence.

But I didn't think so. I was fairly certain it had been a sound jolting me from troubled dreams.

"Ho ooh," called Mr Hoo, and in my somnambulant state I misheard it as 'Uh-oh.'

I struggled to sit up, my heart suddenly beating too quickly, listening out for the tell-tale buzz of spinning red globes. I couldn't hear anything like that. From the floor above me I heard the creaking of floorboards and a toilet flushing.

Was that all? Somebody had visited the bathroom and woken me up.

I let out a shuddering breath, inwardly scolding myself for my overreaction and then lay back down, pulling the quilt over me. The room was cool, the window wide open to allow Mr Hoo free rein to go where he liked overnight. I closed my eyes, seeking a little more blissful sleep.

"Ho ooh."

I opened one eye.

Down the corridor from me, I thought I heard another toilet flush. I frowned.

"Ho ooh."

What? By all that's green?

Footsteps walked across the floor in the room

directly above my head. Was the whole inn awake? Were all of my guests being caught short in the middle of the night?

"Ho ooh."

"Will you stop?" I asked Mr Hoo grumpily, and he made a flapping noise. In the dark his eyes gleamed brightly at me, some sort of smug knowing look there.

I threw back the bedcovers violently, disturbing the air, and he made a leap to the window where he tilted his head as though contemplating how dangerous I was likely to be. At just before three in the morning, the answer was not very.

I pulled on my dressing gown and reached for my wand before padding across the cool floorboards in my bare feet. The nights were getting chiller, and I wished I'd looked for my slippers too.

A momentary silence greeted me outside in the corridor, but the peace only lasted a few seconds before I heard rushing footsteps above, swiftly followed by a groan emanating from a room a little further down from mine. Holding my wand out ready, I relaxed my knees and shoulders and edged forwards. If the inn was being invaded, it was happening on several floors at once.

A brief flash of light in the corner of my eye caught my attention.

I whirled, ready to direct a painful slap of energy at whatever had appeared at the end of the hallway near the stairs, but the pale glow told me it was a ghost.

Florence in fact.

"Hey," I called softly, not wanting to wake any mortals in the inn who might have actually managed to sleep through all the disturbances thus far. "Are you alright?"

She floated towards me, her soft luminescence increasing with every step, the scent of burning cotton never far away.

"I'm fine, Miss Alf." She looked downcast. My stomach squeezed tightly, and my heart ached with disappointment. She was easily the best baker in the competition and yet they'd decided she couldn't participate any further. If I could have reached out and wrapped her in a hug at that moment, I would have done so.

A despairing moan came from behind the door to my right, and I reached out to put my hand on the handle.

"I wouldn't, Miss Alf," Florence warned.

"Somebody might be hurt," I whispered. "Something is going on."

Florence held her hand up. "Wait," she said and walked through the wood of the door as though it wasn't there. She was back a few seconds later, shaking her head and looking a little grim-faced. "It's as I thought. The same as the rest of the inn."

I stared at her, perplexed. What did she mean?

"Food poisoning, Miss Alf. It seems like the whole of the production crew have come down with it."

From the room to the right of me came the sound of the toilet flushing once more. Now I understood. *Ewww.*

I channelled my inner owl. "Ho ooh."

There wasn't an awful lot I could do there and then for anybody, especially at that time of the morning. I went back to bed and lay looking up at the ceiling, listening uneasily to the sounds of an inn more awake than asleep.

Rob's Porky Perfection had to be at the heart of it. I'd arranged catering for everyone from his van. Sausages with either chips or mash, with beans or peas, and gravy. How had it all gone wrong? Rob seemed pernickety in the extreme about hygiene. Had I misjudged and made an entire crew unwell?

Tomorrow I would have to voluntarily call the council to speak to the health department and ask them to investigate. I'd have to double-check that my own kitchen wasn't involved and, given that my chef was both French and a ghost, that experience might verge on the uncomfortable for all concerned.

I wondered if I could secretly pass Charity off as the chef. Would the 'powers that be' buy that?

I'd soon find out.

A headcount the following morning proved my worst suspicions. Those who had chosen to eat at Rob Parker's Porky Perfection van could not make it down to breakfast. Those who had elected to travel into Whittlecombe and eat at The Hay Loft— namely Raoul Scurrysnood and Boo Sully—were perfectly fine.

And then there were those who hadn't eaten at all. Faery Kerry fell into this category because she only ever picked at her food, and a day of tasting bakes rapidly filled her up. There were others who had only eaten a quick sandwich or snack from Whittle Inn's kitchen: Charity, Millicent and I, for example, and there was Patty Cake who had eaten at The Hay Loft and obviously stayed there overnight. We'd all managed to escape.

The only other folk down for breakfast were Murgatroyde Snippe and Bertha. I eyed them suspiciously.

Having decided not to risk asking Rob to cook bacon and sausage in his van, Charity offered them a range of cold breakfast options basically consisting of cereal, fruit and yoghurt.

Clasping a coffee pot in one hand a teapot in the other, I danced between the tables and regarded them all with what I hoped was a mix of professional concern and proof of my capability to deal with any situation.

"Good morning," I greeted them. "I am so sorry about the current situation, but please don't worry. We'll have it investigated and sorted out."

"I'm appalled," Murgatroyde sniffed. "Wait until Patty gets here. She'll have a meltdown."

Raoul tapped Murgatroyde's arm. "It's just one of those things. When you've been involved in the hospitality industry as long as I have, you understand that sometimes these things happen." He looked up at me. "We do all we can, don't we?"

It was nice of him to take my side.

"I'm so glad none of you have been afflicted." I poured tea for Bertha. "You didn't eat at Parker's Porky Perfection?"

Bertha shook her head. "By the time we'd cleaned up the marquee last night, I was dead on my feet. I just went straight to my room and flaked out."

"I'm thankful for that," I said, striving to be sincere. There was something about Bertha that didn't gel. Where once I'd found her friendly and helpful, now I sensed a coldness I couldn't quite figure out.

"And you too, Murgatroyde?" I said, refilling the coffee cup she'd just drained.

"Thank you," she said, and added a couple of teaspoons of sugar, stirring hard. "I was the same. Just wanted to get my head down."

I nodded. Of course. It had been a long tiring day.

"Have you had any more thoughts about Florence?" I asked. "She's devastated to be missing the final."

"None at all," snapped Murgatroyde. "I can't go

against the Witchflix CEO's decision. I value my job far too much."

Raoul looked up at me, his green eyes gleaming. "Rules are rules, Alf. As much as we'd like Florence back, our hands are tied."

I nodded in disappointment and left them to it. As I walked away, I heard Murgatroyde's distinct voice ask, "What are we going to do about filming today if none of the crew are up to it? We're behind schedule as it is. This might mean the bosses cancel *The Great Witchy Cake Off* altogether."

"It won't come to that," Raoul said. "There'll be insurance. We'll just have to wait a day."

"I wouldn't count on it." Murgatroyde's voice was hard and uncompromising. "Hecate only knows what Patty will say. She'll want to sue."

I tutted. Such was the culture we lived in today. Yes, perhaps Witchflix would choose to sue Whittle Inn or even Rob. I doubted poor Rob would be able to afford a lawsuit. I decided I'd better add Penelope Quigwell's name to the list of people I'd be ringing at 9 a.m. to discuss the situation. Forewarned is forearmed, as they say.

Charity caught me as I walked into the kitchen. "Rob's out the back. He's beside himself."

That stood to reason. "Poor man. I'll go and talk

to him and we can make some arrangements to have the health people in."

First though, I put in a quick call to Millicent and asked her to join me at the inn. She'd been intending to come anyway, but I wanted her to bring some supplies. Once I'd had that discussion, I went in search of Rob.

He was waiting for me by the back door, his face ashen. "Alf—" he started to say.

I waved his words away. "Rob," I said as I stopped him. "I know what you're going to say, and I honestly don't believe this is down to you. I'm not sure what's going on, or why, but I'm going to find out."

"But the health authorities—" Rob wrung his hands in agitation.

"I know." I reached out to pat his shoulder. "Look. We're going to play this by the book. I have to get the health authorities involved, because if I don't, likely someone else will and it will just look worse for us. Don't touch anything in your van. Don't clean anything. Don't empty the bins. But trust me, something else is going on here, and we *will* get to the bottom of it."

"You're thinking someone sabotaged me?" Rob asked.

I remembered the weevils in my storerooms and nodded, narrowing my eyes.

"I sure am."

Five minutes later Patty arrived and joined the congregation of judges, presenters and producers at the entrance to the marquee. All hell broke loose when she heard the news that most of her production crew were incapacitated. I rushed over and apologised once again, explaining we were doing all we could to find out the source of the contaminated food that had made everyone ill.

"It's the burger van," Murgatroyde spat. "What else do you possibly need to find out?"

I nodded in agreement. "It certainly looks that way. We'll have the council out later to take a look around it. In the meantime, we're asking everyone to stay away from Rob's place." I smiled. "We don't want to contaminate the contamination."

"What on earth are we going to do?" Patty was asking. "We're due to film the final today, and now we don't have a crew with which to do so." This was true. There were no camera wizards and no sound witches, no make-up, hair or wardrobe.

"Is there no possibility of finding some alternatives?" I asked hopefully. "Shipping them down from the studios in London or Manchester or somewhere?"

"No," Patty wailed. Her face—what I could see of it behind her sunglasses and concealer—appeared pale and drawn. "The big bosses are *not* going to like this. My job could be on the line here. My reputation shot to pieces! The show... the show could be cancelled!"

"Steady, Patty." Raoul, ever the voice of reason, spoke to her gently.

She choked back a sob. "I've worked so hard for so long, but without Janice, it's as though my career is being ripped apart at the seams."

I could taste her despair. My gut feeling was that whatever was happening here was not down to Patty. She genuinely was a hard nut, a tough producer, but she wouldn't have killed Janice, not on purpose. Raoul wrapped his arm around Patty and smiled at me, and I wondered again about his intentions. Would he have reason to sabotage Patty's career by systematically destroying the baking programme she had built up from scratch? He knew Patty better than anyone. He would instinctively understand how difficult she would find it to continue without

Janice as her right-hand woman. Murgatroyde was too much like Patty to make an effective foil.

From the corner of my eye I watched as Ned, freed from his duties to clear up after a minimal breakfast, slunk away from the inn and the gardens heading for Speckled Wood where he would no doubt practise his dancing while Luppitt strummed a madrigal on his lute, and Vance transformed into the largest cheerleader known to witchkind and shook his weighty branches in lieu of pom-poms.

Patty swiped away a tear. "I must deliver this series. There has to be a way to salvage the last programme."

I stared at her thoughtfully, then glanced back at Ned.

"I might just be able to help you with that," I said. "But it'll come at a cost."

CHAPTER FIFTEEN

Whittle Inn bustled with an onset of sudden activity and renewed purpose.

Millicent turned up with a basket full of goodies and began to heat a copper pan full of water over the range. I'd asked her to create a potion that would help to ease the discomfort of all members of the production crew currently smitten by food poisoning. Monsieur Emietter—his redundant knives hanging from their places on the wall—rocked in his chair next to the fire and muttered words I couldn't understand, but they sounded encouraging rather than grumpy so I took that as a good sign.

Silvan, up surprisingly early for once, sprawled on a bench at the kitchen table, despite my insistence that as a paying guest and not a worker he should be in the bar area. He watched the comings and goings with amusement and stared at me insolently every time I had to pass through the kitchen—which was often.

There are times when managing Whittle Inn is akin to directing some oversized opera, and today was going to be one such instance. I had a plan, and now I had to find a way to put it into practice.

Millicent was the first part, but the second part involved the Devonshire Fellows. Fortunately for me, the entire travelling band of Elizabethan minstrels were all in residence. Fortune is a double-edged sword, of course, because at least when they were out on tour, the inn was spared their rambunctious cacophony.

In addition to Luppitt Smeatharpe, the Devonshire Fellows were made up of lute player Robert Wait, the leader of the group; William Wait, his brother and main fiddle player; Napier Harrow, a percussionist; John Bond, the second fiddle; and Stephen Arcott, who played a variety of wind instruments—most of which sounded like a goose objecting to being squeezed hard around its middle.

After searching the inn and the grounds and sending Zephaniah out into the wood to locate Luppitt, I finally gathered them all together in the kitchen.

"I need your help," I announced when I'd

managed to get them all to lay down their instruments for just two minutes.

"Anything." Robert smiled solicitously, giving a little bow. The others grouped behind him, looking at each other with raised eyebrows.

"That depends what it is, rightfully," suggested John Bond, but Luppitt shushed him.

"We'll do anything for you, my lady," he said, and there were more nods.

"Be it a gala you'd like us to play at?" asked Napier with enthusiasm. "A wedding party to serenade?"

"Ah... er... no. It's a bit different to that. Erm..." I coughed nervously. "In fact, it won't involve using your instruments at all."

Thank goodness.

"Aww," Napier said, and there were general murmurings of discontent from the others too. I needed to repackage my offer quickly and make it more attractive.

"Better than that!" I injected an air of excitement into my voice to mask my desperation. "It's a professional gig. Working with the television show producers who've been staying at the inn this past week or so."

I expected that the Devonshire Fellows—given

the time period in which they'd died—wouldn't really understand about television and how it worked, but I was hoping they understood the entertainment aspect of it.

"*The Great Witchy Cake Off*?" William asked in surprise.

They *had* heard of it. They'd obviously been hanging around Florence. "That's the one," I said.

"Presenting?" asked Robert hopefully.

"Can I be a judge?" Napier asked, wiggling his fingers in anticipation.

From the direction of the kitchen table came a snort of amusement. Silvan.

"Nothing like that," I said, ignoring the dark wizard. The ghosts twisted their faces and looked a little downcast. "But far better! I know you're all adept at what you do, and I need you to transfer those skills. I want you to operate the cameras and the sound and help us finish the show today."

"Oooh." Robert sucked in air over his teeth. "That sounds complicated."

"It is a *little* complicated," I admitted. "But we're going to use magick to help you, and in combination with your own dexterity, I know you'll make this a success."

Robert looked around at the others. Luppitt

smiled up at me. For him it was a no-brainer. He'd always do anything he could to assist me, and I loved him for that. "Of course we will, my lady!" he chipped in before anybody else could raise any more objections. "We'd love to do it, wouldn't we fellows?"

Caught up in Luppitt's excitement, the other ghosts nodded their heads. When Napier began to beat out a rhythm on his drum to express his newfound enthusiasm, I exited the kitchen in a hurry. "See you in the marquee in fifteen minutes," I called back over my shoulder, and left Silvan to enjoy the raucous merrymaking and dubious musicality of my band of minstrels.

Florence appeared inside the marquee looking doubtful, as well she might.

I smiled encouragement and beckoned her over.

"I shouldn't be here, Miss," she told me nervously.

"It's absolutely fine. I've cut a bit of a deal with Patty."

Florence glanced around nervously as Eloise and Scampi took their places in the kitchen. "What sort of a deal?"

I took a deep breath. "In order to work all the technical equipment today, I've persuaded Patty that we should be allowed to use magick. Let's face it, Bertha and Boo are witches with a good knowledge of how all this technical malarkey works—the cameras and microphones and recording equipment and so on. With them in overall control and with help from Ross Baines—"

Florence's eyes sparkled at the mention of his name.

"And with Robert Wait as assistant director to replace Jemima, we'll use magick to help the rest of the Devonshire Fellows move the cameras around and record everything." As I spoke, the Devonshire Fellows entered the marquee and looked around in awe at the equipment they would be dealing with. Ross Baines followed closely behind them, and I waved at him.

"Ross can help make sure that everything is recorded all day long, and Millicent is working on a quick cure that will have the rest of the production crew up and about in no time at all. They'll take over when they can, but at any rate, they'll have plenty of material to work with when it comes to editing."

Florence smiled but looked confused. "I'm very

pleased to hear that, Miss Alf, but where do I come in?"

"I promised Patty Cake I could make this work," I told my housekeeper, gesturing around at the cameras and equipment. "And in return, I asked that you be reinstated."

"Reinstated—" Florence stared at me through wide eyes.

"Yes. I said we would pull out all the stops to finish the filming today, but only if you were allowed to compete."

Florence gasped. "I don't know what to say, Miss Alf."

I dropped my voice. "Florence," I said kindly. "There's one more thing. They did agree to let you compete, but I had to agree that they won't allow you to win. It doesn't matter how well you do today, they will only get this programme—and therefore the whole series—past the big bosses at Witchflix *as long as a witch wins the overall competition*. Do you understand?"

Florence caught her breath and my eyes moistened. Of course it was unfair, but life is a series of negotiations—and for now, this was the best I could do for her.

"Are you asking me to throw the competition, Miss Alf?"

"No. I most certainly am not." I studied her seriously. "I am telling you to cook your heart out and do Whittle Inn proud."

Florence raised her chin and her eyes cleared. As always, she floored me with her positivity. "That sounds like the perfect solution, Miss Alf." She grinned. "So what if I can't win? It's the participation that counts. I'm going to knock their socks off."

"Get to it!" I nodded.

While Florence, who of course hadn't thought to prepare a menu for her day's baking, pored over her hastily scrambled together plan of action, I helped Patty and Boo brief the Devonshire Fellows and Ross on what they would be doing. I'd suggested Ross should be in charge of digital editing, and so to that end, he would be monitoring the digital takes throughout the filming and making sure they were stored properly for retrieval by the production's own editors when they felt better.

We'd assigned Robert Wait the task of assisting Boo Sully with the direction as the Devonshire

Fellows tended to listen to him, and he could be authoritative in a calm manner. We'd made the fiddle players William and John, along with Luppitt, the camera operators, leaving Stephen and Napier to work as sound engineers. They were all good musicians, so I had made the—not unreasonable—assumption that they would have a keen eye for detail and would work quickly and nimbly.

I'd volunteered Charity to assist with clearing the set and supporting Bertha with her workload, and I intended to jump in as and when I could. For now, I needed to leave them to it. My next port of call had to be the officials from the gas company, so I made my excuses, promised to return as quickly as bureaucracy allowed and high-tailed it down the drive and along my narrow lane to where they were digging up the road.

I slowed to a trot, recognising the indolent whistling I could hear as I approached the junction between Whittle Inn and the road. I wasn't surprised when Silvan pushed himself away from one of the large old oak trees that lined the lane and fell in beside me.

"Don't you have anything else to do rather than stalk me when I'm working?" I asked.

He flashed me that impudent smile I knew so

well. "You're working, are you? I assumed you were fire-fighting."

I tutted and shook my head, unsure of the difference. Trying to move faster, I hoped he'd take the message and leave me to it, but he matched my pace and began whistling again, only stopping when we reached the place where the workmen were digging.

"How's it going?" I asked an official-looking man with a clipboard, the one who'd spoken to me the day before.

"It's the strangest thing," he said, pushing his too-large yellow helmet away from his eyebrows. "We thought we had a blockage here yesterday, but overnight, we've been monitoring it and it seems to be perfectly fine."

"The blockage is unblocked?" Silvan asked.

The official looked from me to Silvan and back again. "That's about the size of it."

"So we have gas at the inn now?" I asked with relief.

"Yes. It should all be back to normal." The official pointed at the digger parked by the side of the road. "We'll refill the hole and with any luck, you shouldn't have any more trouble."

"That's great news," I smiled. One problem solved at least.

"So, what caused the blockage?" asked Silvan, leaning forward to look in the hole as though he'd be able to diagnose the issue simply by looking.

The official shook his head. "To be honest, your guess is as good as mine. I've never seen anything like it before."

"Hmm." Silvan stroked his chin. "A blockage that unblocks all by itself on the morning after the night before."

I shifted my weight uneasily. I could see what he was getting at. The official looked worried, like he thought he'd done something wrong. I quickly sought to reassure him. "I'm just glad that all's well that ends well," I told him.

Silvan dropped to his knees and stuck his head in the hole. I noticed him make a swift movement with his right hand that anybody else might have missed. Then he jumped up and took my arm to pull me away.

I turned to wave my thanks at the official as Silvan marched me back up the lane.

"All's well that ends well? Maybe so, Alf. But it hasn't ended yet, has it?"

A car with the local council's official logo appeared at the end of the lane and trundled towards us. The health department. I waved at them, my heart sinking when I recognised who they were. I pulled my arm loose from Silvan and beckoned the occupants of the car to follow me to the inn, uttering a little prayer spell as I walked. "Goddess Endovelicus, it if pleases you to hear my plea, I beg that you please let this visitation go well for me and exonerate both Whittle Inn and poor Rob. I bask in your blessings. So mote it be."

"Well amen to that." Silvan smirked, and I nudged him hard with my elbow and turned to face the newcomers.

"We need to talk, Alf," Silvan called as I walked away from him.

"I'll catch up with you in a little while," I promised, then offered my full and solemn attention to the man and woman in front of me, because after all, they had the power to shut down the inn once and for all.

Less than an hour later I was back in the marquee and the pair from the health department had taken their samples and left. They'd seemed decent enough and had put Rob at his ease. They could see how clean and tidy he kept everything, and his van was practically new anyway. They expressed the wish that the samples they'd taken from the food stored in his fridges, coupled with samples from the rubbish, would quickly tell them what had happened.

I had a strong suspicion it wouldn't, but at least I'd done all the right things and made all the correct noises. I'd opened the kitchen and my storerooms to them—having shooed Monsieur Emietter and all my other ghosts away, but they had merely taken a cursory look around and shone their torches into the corners and under the kitchen cabinets, taking a few swabs, collecting some brushings here and there, before bagging everything up, labelling the evidence, thanking me and leaving.

"Cut! Cut!" Boo was screaming as I entered the tent.

"Cut!" Robert Wait echoed.

Neither of them could hear themselves above the high levels of volume in the tent. Total hilarity. Not what I'd come to expect of *The Great Witchy Cake Off,* which was gentle and funny in a quiet chuckle kind of way.

Until today, apparently.

I'd left Bertha, Patty and Boo to sort out the magick that would be needed to assist my ghosts in the operation of the large cameras and the sound equipment, but now I watched in horror as Luppitt and William flew through the air, riding the cameras as though they were broomsticks, to take close-up shots of the contestants as they decorated their signature bakes.

Finbarr's pixies had somehow made it into the tent, although the Irish witch was himself nowhere to be seen. I curled my toes in horror as half a dozen pixies, armed with piping bags, tried to ice each other with brightly coloured frostings. The other half dozen had made a sandpit from a large bag of flour and were throwing flour bombs at each other.

Napier, meanwhile, was experimenting with percussion noises by recording the sound that eggs make when you throw them into a glass bowl set on the floor from a height of approximately six feet, while Bertha tried to wrestle the huge furry microphone—now covered in eggshell and splatterings of yolk—from him. Stephen Arcott played the recording back at a high volume for everyone in the tent to hear, turning up the trebles just to make us all wince some more. Patty clasped her hands to her cheeks in despair.

"Stop! Stop!" she was shrieking.

"Cut!" Boo yelled.

"Cut! Cut!" parroted Robert Wait, but to no effect. The ghosts wilfully ignored him.

Raoul and Faery Kerry had retired to wherever it was the judges retire to when they weren't needed and only Mindi, hovering in the background, appeared to be taking everything in her stride. "I don't think you should really be doing that," she remarked mildly, as Luppitt soared past her and one of the pixies skidded over on a patch of spilt egg.

My stomach lurched as I took in all that was going on, then tipped over when I watched Murgatroyde Snippe pull her mobile phone from her pocket. I knew what she would do. She would phone the big bosses and tell them.

Because—I realised with a jolt—unlike everyone else working on *The Great Witchy Cake Off*, that's the sort of person she was. A mean-spirited tittle-tattle who put herself above the programme everyone else worked so hard to create.

Murgatroyde tapped something out on her phone.

Somewhere to the left of me, hidden by a wall of computer screens, Ross made a sound as though he had stubbed his toe, but he was the least of my worries.

Knowing the ban on magick in the marquee had

been lifted, I directed a slither of annoyed energy Murgatroyde's way. *"Prohibere,"* I ordered, keeping my voice low and my tone pleasant. I watched as Murgatroyde tapped the phone and glared at it, then lifted it up, the universal movement of someone looking for a signal.

As Luppitt flew straight for me, an alarming sight given the size of the camera he sat astride, I held up my hand as though to catch him. He came to a rapid halt and was ejected over the top of the boom handle. Being a ghost he couldn't hurt himself when he landed, but I heartily wished I could have given him a kick in the pants for his trouble.

The other ghosts, realising playtime was up, stopped what they were doing and sheepishly avoided my gaze.

"For shame," I said to Luppitt, then raised my voice to take all of the culprits in. "For shame, all of you! I asked you to do one thing for me and I turned my back for a few minutes—"

"More like an hour," grumbled Murgatroyde. "I knew this was a bad idea—"

I spoke over her. "I turn my back, and this is what you do? Do you know how much work goes into making a programme like this? Do you have any idea what you are doing to each baker's concentration? They can't re-bake their goodies. This is a competition. This is their one shot." I scowled at the Devonshire Fellows. "Listen, if you're not up to the task, I'll find someone else and you can go back to the shadows and work on your madrigals."

"I'm sure they won't be any more palatable," Ross said softly from his corner. "Alf, I really need to talk to you."

"One sec—"

"Oh! I knew this wasn't going to work," Murgatroyde screeched loudly, and we all turned towards her. "The programme is ruined. They'll fire me. They'll fire us all! I can't bear it! My heart!" she howled and then fainted dead away.

You can imagine the fuss. We all crowded around her, instinctively trying to offer assistance while simultaneously denying her the opportunity to find oxygen.

Patty clasped her head as though it was about to explode. "Can this get any worse?" she cried, and I had to sympathise. Chaos. Chaos everywhere.

I yelled for Finbarr and he ran in to retrieve his pixies. I rolled my eyes as he made his apologies, wondering whether the time had come to send him home. Meanwhile, we'd called Millicent down from the inn to assist us. She'd been offering solace and magickal remedies to those afflicted by food poisoning. Honestly, I could have reconfigured the marquee to use as a hospital tent, such did Whittle Inn feel like a war zone at that moment. Millicent, as always, brooked no nonsense, and once order had been restored and Murgatroyde had been fortified with green tea and a little something extra that Millicent had added to help calm her down, I turned to the Devonshire Fellows who were patiently—and shame-facedly—awaiting instructions.

Given the interminable delays, we were way behind schedule, so I mouthed a hurried apology to Ross as Boo set the cameras rolling once more. I'd catch up with him a little later.

The theme for the final *Cake Off* show of the series was Halloween. Fitting, because it would be aired on October 31.

Boo called action, and Bertha re-invoked the spell that would start the cameras rolling. Luppitt, William and John just had to move them around and change the focus of attention occasionally. As long as everything was held steady and we had plenty of footage for the editors at the end of the day, everything would work out fine. Similarly, Stephen and Napier had to be in the right place at the right time to pick up the sound on their microphones and keep a check on the levels. Ross, behind the scenes, was monitoring for overall sound levels and background noise as well as keeping an eye on what we were filming.

Or at least I hoped he was. He had his head down and his brow was furrowed with concentration, so that was something.

As Boo sent in Mindi to chat with Scampi, I craned my neck to have a look at Florence's signature bake. This first challenge asked for two dozen fairy cakes for a child's party. Florence had opted to create twelve 'good fairy' and twelve 'evil fairy' cakes, possibly inspired by my tale of woe from the previous Christmas. The twelve good fairy cakes were created using an almond sponge mix, flavoured with a tiny amount of sloe berry. I could see her now applying pure white frosting flavoured with lemon to these and carefully crafting wings from edible rice paper. Her other batch of cakes were bright red.

As Mindi counted down to the end, the contestants placed their bakes on the end of their benches. Raoul and Faery Kerry went around to each to look, sniff and taste each batch.

Eloise was up first, and to be fair what she had looked good, but unfortunately, she hadn't had time to finish the icing of the second batch, so she hadn't finished the task completely. Scampi fared even worse. He'd managed to produce twenty-four cakes, but they hadn't held their shape under the weight of the toppings, and several of them collapsed as the judges approached.

Finally it was Florence's turn. Some of the fairies had been finished off in a rush and their faces were lopsided, but otherwise the cakes looked great. The delicate rice paper fairy wings had been brushed with edible gold shimmer and tiny silver balls. Her red cakes, decorated with little figures that looked like demons with fairy wings, had a chilli chocolate topping and gold ball decorations.

"Well, I think they look amazing, Florence," Faery Kerry was saying.

"I wouldn't like to meet some of the faeries you're acquainted with," Raoul chipped in, and Florence laughed.

"The flavours are impressive. The chilli isn't too overpowering at all," Faery Kerry said, nibbling on the frosting.

"I agree. I think you've done a great job here, Florence. Well done!"

Florence beamed into the camera and gave a thumbs up.

Boo called cut.

"We'll just have a short break and go straight on to the next round," he announced. "Clear everything down and set up for the technical challenge, please."

"Clear down," repeated Robert Wait, full of his own self-importance as assistant director.

"Clear down," repeated Bertha, and shot Robert an annoyed look. My Wonky Inn Ghostly Clean-Up Crew leapt to the challenge, scurrying around the set, spiriting the used pots, pans, bowls, plates and utensils away and replacing them with fresh ones, sweeping, cleaning, even scrubbing surfaces clean where necessary.

I needed a cup of tea and wanted to check on whether Millicent's potion had started to work on the production crew, but Charity grabbed me before I could get very far. "George is here," she told me, so I went to find him.

He was waiting for me at the bar, chatting with Zephaniah. Given how quiet it had been over breakfast there hadn't been a huge amount of clearing up to do, and, at a loose end, Zephaniah had been completing a crossword—something he was a huge fan of.

"Eat something quickly?" Zephaniah was asking George.

"How many letters?" George frowned.

Zephaniah checked. "Five."

"Five? Gobble?"

"That's six," I interrupted them. "G.O.B.B.L.E." I counted the letters off on my fingers. "Six."

"So what's the answer then, Ms Clever Clogs?" George asked.

I laughed. "At least I can count, Detective Sergeant Gilchrist."

"But you don't know the answer, do you?" George smiled.

"Eat something quickly?" I thought for a moment. "How about fast?" George roared with laughter.

"That's four letters!"

I rolled my eyes. "Oh yeah. You got me on that one. I was thinking 'quickly' means fast, and you can fast instead of feast." I pulled him away from Zephaniah. "Anyway... do you have any news?"

George shook his head. "Nope. Nothing at all. What about you? What about Ross?"

Ross. Oh yes. Oops. I'd been meaning to have a word with him. "He did want to talk to me, so I'd better catch up with him. I think he may have something for us."

"Feast?" said Zephaniah in the background, thinking aloud.

"Can we talk to him now?" George asked, meaning Ross.

"He's tied up in the marquee at the moment," I said, and George looked puzzled.

"Ross is in the marquee? Is he taking part?"

"Just don't ask," I said. "It's been crazy here."

"When isn't it crazy here?" George muttered.

I folded my arms in defence. "I'll drag him out as soon as they finish filming the morning session. Shouldn't be too much longer."

"Morning!" Marissa entered the bar with Silvan not far behind her. "Nice to see you again, DS Gilchrist."

George perked up at the sight of Marissa. Today she'd dressed in a sky-blue silk shift that shimmered as she walked. With her white hair tumbling over her shoulders, she looked like a goddess. Even I sighed at the sight of her.

"I told you, Marissa, please call me George," George said.

Silvan sidled up to me and I thought he was going to make some cutting remark about George's propensity to chat up other women, or my inability to keep a love interest for very long, but he held himself in check.

"A curious thing," he said, leaning close and speaking low. "I've just seen someone using the phone in your office when they thought no-one was looking."

"I don't mind if someone needs to use a phone." I dismissed the information, assuming he meant Charity or Millicent.

"Even one of the guests?" Silvan asked.

"Who?"

"The little producer."

"Murgatroyde?" I asked, and Silvan shrugged. "Small woman, short dark hair, wears men's suits?"

Silvan smiled. "That's the one. Why would she have needed to use the phone in your office?"

"Because I blocked all the phones in the marquee," I explained. "I think she was about to call the producers and tell them what a mess the filming is." I wondered if she had now called them. Why hadn't she asked for permission to use my phone? Why the secrecy?

More importantly, they'd be on to Patty if they were unhappy. This could all end in disaster.

Next to us, George had engaged Marissa in

conversation and was obviously trying to wow her with his intellect. "I was just helping Zephaniah with his crossword," he told her. "Are you any good at crosswords? What was that clue again, Zeph?"

Zephaniah consulted the grid. "Seven down. Eat something quickly."

"Hmmm," Marissa said. "Are there any letter clues?"

Zephaniah unfolded his newspaper to show her the grid. There was a photo of Janice standing with Raoul, Patty and Faery Kerry on the reverse. It had been taken by the local press on the day they had arrived. "Second letter 'c'."

Second letter c?

Eat something quickly?

Murgatroyde.

The image of Janice in the paper pulsed and vibrated as I stared at it. My brain began to whir, filling in missing letters, and the missing pieces of a puzzle too.

How had I missed something so blindingly obvious?

"George! I need to show you something!"

CHAPTER SIXTEEN

We had some parts of the puzzle, but we didn't have them all. I took George up to Murgatroyde's room and he made a swift but thorough search of it, bagging a few items in plastic evidence bags, and then mob-handed—because Silvan insisted on coming along too—we returned to the marquee where filming had wrapped up for the morning.

George entered the tent first, holding his badge up so that everyone could see he was on official business. Most people were present, with the exception of Patty and Bertha. I assumed they were collecting production notes and directions for the final part of filming.

It didn't matter.

It wasn't them we were interested in.

"Ladies and gentlemen, if you could all remain

where you are please." He looked at me. "Except the ghosts, Alf."

"Okay, guys," I told the Devonshire Fellows. "Why don't you take a break and I'll call you back when we're ready to resume." If we were ever ready to resume. Things looked kind of bleak.

I asked Florence to stay, though, and given that Ross was waving at me, I figured he had something to say to me too, so I didn't banish him.

"Ms Snippe," George began, "I have a few questions I'd like to ask you. Can we step aside—"

"Me?" Murgatroyde asked, and her face flushed. "What do you want with me? I haven't done anything."

"I'm sure that's the case," George said pleasantly. "I just need to ask—"

Murgatroyde rolled her fists into tightly clenched balls of fury. "No! I'm not feeling well." Her voice rose. "Leave me alone. You've nothing on me!"

George looked alarmed and turned to me. "You said she hadn't been feeling well. Is she—"

"Batpoop!" Millicent exclaimed as Murgatroyde clutched her chest. "I gave her enough stimulant in her anti-fainting potion to keep a horse awake for a week."

Murgatroyde glared at Millicent. "What are you saying? Have you poisoned me? I'll take legal action."

"Is that all you think about?" Millicent folded her arms. "Sue away. The only thing I have of value is my dogs, and even they're a pair of mongrels."

"This is a conspiracy!" Murgatroyde shrieked, and I frowned at her ridiculously melodramatic over-reaction. Why was she being so loud? What was wrong with the woman?

"DS Gilchrist just wants to ask a few questions," I reminded her, trying to stay calm. "You're not under arrest. You weren't even here when Janice was—"

Around us, the walls of the marquee jittered as though caught by a heavy wind. I turned my head in surprise. Until now, they'd hardly flapped at all.

"Look out!" shouted Raoul, and I heard Faery Kerry scream.

A whisper of wind and something dark flew past me, temporarily clouding my vision. I ducked and at the same time was pulled off my feet, landing on my hands and knees on the makeshift floor of the tent. There was a clunk and a howl of pain to the side of me, and I spun sideways, jumping to my feet as Silvan had taught me to do.

Silvan!

He lay on the floor, sprawled on top of George, but it was George who was howling. One of the main joists that held the marquee together had come loose and swung free, and while Silvan had managed to jump to George's aid, the joist had still connected with George's shoulder.

Better that than his head, I supposed.

"My goodness," Mindi spoke softly. "Such drama."

"Is everyone alright?" I asked as Millicent rushed to George's side.

"Argh!" George moaned in agony.

Millicent knelt beside the injured detective. "Don't worry," she told him, "I know a little spell to take the pain away, and then we'll get you to a hospital."

"Not so fast." Murgatroyde pulled out a wand and waved it at me. "Give me the evidence bags."

I stared at her in shock.

"Don't do that, Alf," George said through gritted teeth.

"Do it, or I'll loosen another joist." Murgatroyde wagged her wand at me. "And the next one won't miss."

From the floor, I watched with one eye as Silvan casually reached into his pocket. He slowly drew his wand out, but before he could do anything, a hot flash of energy forked through the air from behind me and knocked it away.

I swivelled in surprise.

Bertha had sneaked into the marquee and was now standing behind Ross. In one hand she held out her own wand, and in the other she had a vial of water poised in the air above the ghost's head.

"Holy water," she told me. "From the font in the local church."

She stood there, confident, ready to drip the water onto Ross. She had to imagine she could banish him using an exorcism of some kind.

I calculated the risk and decided we were on dicey ground. I couldn't be sure what would happen if she dropped that water on Ross's head.

I'd had my suspicions about Bertha for a while, but I didn't understand her link to Murgatroyde or why either of them would have wanted Janice Tork-Mimosa dead.

"Hand me the evidence bags, Alf," Murgatroyde repeated, "and then nobody needs to get hurt."

From above came the sound of another large joist creaking. Outside, a guy line twanged. The sides of the marquee flapped ominously. What could I do? Reluctantly, I bent over and picked up two of the three evidence bags that had spilled onto the floor when George had been knocked flying. The third had landed near Silvan. I glanced from it to him. We locked eyes. I rolled my left shoulder back slightly, indicating Bertha with her vial poised above poor Ross's head. I blinked twice, and an understanding passing between us.

Silvan reached for the third bag and held it out to me. I pretended not to see him doing this. Instead, I stood slowly and held up the two bags I'd already picked up, allowing Murgatroyde to see them clearly.

Timing was everything.

As Murgatroyde reached to take the bags from me, I threw them straight at her face, bent my knees and spun around. Using one hand, I sent a blast at the space Bertha had been inhabiting. She'd obviously anticipated something would happen because she'd side-stepped. Instantly she tried to fire back at me. I deflected and rapidly sent a heat spell her way. It obliterated her vial of water, the glass cracking in her hand and the water turning to a puff of steam that rose harmlessly into the air.

"Go!" I shouted at Ross, and he took the hint, apparating safely out of harm's way as the vial shattered on the ground where he'd been a moment before.

Meanwhile, at the same time that I'd thrown my evidence bags, Silvan tossed his own at Murgatroyde, confusing her as to the direction of each threat. She struck out blindly, her magick awry. While I concentrated on Bertha, still armed with her own wand, Silvan piled pressure on Murgatroyde, who shied away from his advances.

I'd like to say Murgatroyde was no match for a dark wizard, someone as well-practised in the dark arts as Silvan, and to be fair, she probably wasn't. But funnily enough, it was mild-mannered Mindi who came to our rescue.

"For heaven's sake," I heard her mutter. She raised her arms and clapped, just once, and the next second, the cameras were flying through the air of their own accord. One took out Bertha with a hefty clunk to the side of her head, and the other toppled onto Murgatroyde, pinning her to the ground. "That'll do it," Mindi said mildly. "I'm off for a cigarette break."

I jumped on top of Bertha, shoving my knee into her solar plexus, grappling with her to retrieve her wand. When I snapped it into several pieces and dashed it to the floor, she glared at me with unconcealed hatred.

"Why did you have to interfere?" she spat. "We had it all figured out."

I shrugged. "Then you shouldn't have brought your baking programme to Whittle Inn. We don't suffer fools—or murderers—gladly here."

CHAPTER SEVENTEEN

We gathered together in the bar awaiting a couple of George's team to arrive to sort out the arrests. George had his arm in a sling, and Millicent hovered over him with concern, her pain-alleviating spell already kicking in. Silvan had a beauty of a black eye. I wasn't sure whether the joist had caught him, or George had—either way, it was going to look spectacular. Raoul and Faery Kerry, looking a little shaken, sat with Mindi, Patty and Boo. Ross hovered by the bar, his laptop set up, and flicked through endless screens collating evidence of the information he had gleaned.

George had handcuffed the producer and Bertha together, the cuffs laced between the back of their chairs. They weren't going anywhere in a hurry. The evidence bags lay on a table in front of me. The most important of these, the *scarf*—or Zephaniah's 'seven down crossword clue', as I'd always think of it in the future—had finally given the game away. I'd seen it under Murgatroyde's bed, hidden in her suitcase, but actually, it had been Janice's. I'd seen her wearing it, and the photo in the paper had reminded me of that. I held up the bag to show Murgatroyde.

"This could have been a simple coincidence," I said. "Yes, we found this scarf under your bed, and it's the same as the one I'd seen Janice wearing, but there's no reason why two women wouldn't have similar scarves. Janice was a classy woman. When I first saw this, I imagined you were trying to emulate her. We only wanted to ask you about it. If you hadn't overreacted when we brought it into the marquee, we might have never progressed any further."

Silvan grunted. "The reaction was fake, wasn't it? I'm guessing you were trying to alert Bertha to your predicament. You needed her help, and she wasn't in the tent at the time. But she came running when you yelled."

Murgatroyde ignored Silvan and glared at George instead. "I didn't kill Janice, and you can't prove I did."

"I know. You hadn't even arrived at Whittle-combe. We had Ross check out the CCTV at

Paddington Station. It showed you getting on the train in London and arriving into Exeter. The time frame clearly demonstrates you arrived after the murder. It was the perfect alibi." George pointed at Ross's screen. Divided into quarters, we had four pictures of Murgatroyde on the platform in London, on the train, alighting at Exeter and getting into a taxi outside the station in Exeter at around the time Janice was murdered. The time stamps gave her the alibis she needed.

"It could also have been a coincidence that you were already on your way down to Devon. Almost as though you knew the programme would require another producer," George said. "But I don't think so. How could you have known that in advance?"

"I just wanted to see how things were going with the programme."

"Well, I'll definitely be asking your bosses whether they had given you prior permission to come down here to Devon, but my instinct says they only agreed to you being here after Janice had been murdered."

"But I didn't kill Janice," Murgatroyde repeated doggedly. "You can't make that stick."

"We will however prove conspiracy to murder. You'll go down for a long, long time." George nodded, entirely self-assured. "It might go easier for you if you just spill the beans. How did you persuade Bertha to do your bidding?"

"No comment." Murgatroyde sat back in her seat and stared up at the ceiling.

"I think I might be able to help with that." Ross's quiet voice drifted among us. "Bertha Crumb is a pseudonym for Bertha Louise Sawley, who was born to Murgatroyde Jane Snippe nee Sawley on 29th May 1994."

I did a double take. Mother and daughter? I'd never have imagined Murgatroyde was old enough to be Bertha's mother, and I couldn't see a resemblance. But then there was all the make-up she was constantly covered with. Murgatroyde could have been an alien from another planet and I might not have been able to tell, given her obsession with concealer and all manner of cosmetics. Her filthy room lay as testament to that.

"Murgatroyde Jane Snippe, date of birth 11th November 1967."

Early fifties? I blew out my cheeks. I'd thought she was my age. Maybe I needed to learn contouring or something.

"They were working together?" asked Patty, and George nodded. Patty slid an elegant finger underneath her glasses to wipe at a tear. "Poor, poor Janice. She thought Bertha was a hard worker. She often praised her. Said she'd like to progress her career." She peered over her sunglasses at Bertha. "How could you do that to her?"

Bertha fidgeted in her seat, and Murgatroyde shot her a warning glance.

"I didn't realise it was Janice."

There was a shocked silence in the marquee. Bertha's face collapsed in sorrow. "We were after Patty!"

"You were trying to kill Ms Cake?" George sought clarification.

Bertha let out a noisy, wet sob. "It was normally Patty who checked on the set first thing in the morning. I'd been waiting for her."

"But Patty was staying at The Hay Loft and she needed to wait for Raoul to give her a lift back here," I said.

Patty opened and closed her mouth, stunned beyond words.

"Oh my," said Faery Kerry on Patty's behalf.

"So, it was a case of mistaken identities," George said. "That doesn't carry any less of a penalty, I'm afraid."

"What do you have against Patty?" Raoul

wanted to know. "It's thanks to her we have jobs at all."

Bertha looked down at her feet. Murgatroyde glared at Raoul and refused to answer.

"What I don't understand, is why you bothered with all the theatrics? Why stab her with a cake knife when you could have used a hex?" Mindi asked them both, her face doleful. "You're witches. You could just throw a curse out and have done with it."

"That's what I wanted to do!" Bertha said. "But mother said we needed to make it look like some mortal had done it."

"Bertha!" Murgatroyde warned her daughter.

"Oh, Mother, they know most of it anyway." Bertha glowered back at her.

"You were trying to frame Rob Parker," I said. "Conveniently, he'd had a little run-in with Janice on that first afternoon. Nothing serious, but witnessed by several people."

Something twisted in my stomach as I thought through the chain of events. "You put Rob in the frame for it, but you didn't care who else you hurt along the way. You planted the weevils in my store-room, thinking you'd alert the health department to issues with hygiene at the inn. Unfortunately for you, we nipped that in the bud before you could process a complaint. So then you had to frame Rob."

"Perhaps you were trying to contaminate his fridges or the food itself when we spotted your djinn that night we came home late from The Hay Loft," Silvan suggested, "and you abandoned the attempt."

Bertha shrugged. "I realised not enough people would be made sick, because only a few of the crew chose to eat from the sausage van on any one night. The food at the inn was far too good and most of the crew wanted to eat here."

"So you sabotaged the gas supply." Silvan nodded knowingly. "I found elements of magick in the hole where the gas workers were digging. I knew there'd been some sort of interference."

Of course. That's what he'd been checking for. "You two purposefully blocked the gas at the entrance to the inn, forcing the closure of our kitchen?" I asked.

"Knowing that you'd use Rob for everybody's dinner," Silvan confirmed.

Dastardly, as my great-grandmother would say.

"Then either Bertha or Murgatroyde contaminated something in Rob's van and, completely innocent, he served up everyone's sausages." Fury burned in my veins. "You took an innocent woman's life and you may have ruined an innocent man's livelihood! Don't you care at all?"

Murgatroyde shrugged. "It would have been worth it," she said, "if it had killed Patty's career stone dead."

She rocked forward on her chair, her face twisting with hatred. "Patty, Patty, Patty! Always blasted Patty getting all the jobs and making all the decisions. I'm just as good a producer as she is, but do you think I can get work? No! I hate her." She spat at Patty, who recoiled from the onslaught. "Do you hear me? I hate you!"

"So that's what it was all about," I said, after Bertha and Murgatroyde had been taken away to the police station in Exeter. "They just wanted to ruin Patty's career."

"Patty and Murgatroyde have been rivals for years," said Mindi. "Patty's star has always shone more brightly than Murgatroyde's, and the shows she's produced have reaped big rewards for Witch-flix. She's the mighty Witchflix producer of choice for a range of baking and reality programmes because everything she touches turns to gold."

"Perhaps Murgatroyde didn't think she could get a look-in," Faery Kerry suggested, her face downcast.

"That's no reason to kill someone," Raoul replied, and his eyes had lost their twinkle. "She was a decent woman, Janice. She should have lived out her life in peace."

We all nodded in agreement, mourning a life wasted. Then Ross quietly interjected. "I found your videos, Raoul." He looked at me. "While I was in the marquee, Bertha managed to send a text before you killed her phone. That brief signal was enough for me to triangulate her phone and log it. With that data, I managed a definite hit. It was her phone that had sent video messages to Raoul."

"And were they the genuine article?" Raoul asked.

"No." Ross shook his head, an emphatic denial. "Most certainly not. The images were of Janice, and there were images of Pierre de Corduroy, but they had been manipulated. It's not at all difficult these days to do that with the range of software that's widely available, but these had been enhanced magickly. It was impressive and convincing. Murgatroyde had managed to make a whole film. Fairly indecent. Utterly immoral." Ross wiped his hands on his trousers in distaste.

"So Janice wasn't having an affair." Raoul looked troubled. "I gave her a hard time about that, but she was blameless all along."

"Anybody in your shoes might have done the same," I said. "Between them, Murgatroyde and Bertha had plenty of skills. They knew what they were doing. They manipulated a great many people."

"It's a pity we didn't see through them," Faery Kerry said.

Raoul nodded. "We just have to be thankful that Silvan, Alf and George did. At least they've saved Patty's career from almost certain implosion."

Patty stared at us, then slowly reached up to remove her dark sunglasses. Beneath them, her eyes were oddly soft, a glorious chocolate brown colour. "You've done me a huge favour," she said. "I won't forget it. Thank you, Wilf."

CHAPTER EIGHTEEN

By the time filming started on the final showstopper of the series, it was past five o'clock. The challenge was due to last three hours, so we were heading for a late finish. I watched as Florence put her head down over her ingredients and started cooking up a storm. I couldn't wait to see what she would conjure up.

Conjure without using magick of course, because that—as we all know—would have been cheating.

And now we had to abide by the very letter of the rules, because we had several new guests. It turned out that Murgatroyde had managed to contact the producers in a final text sent before I could block it, and they had suddenly turned up at Whittle Inn without warning.

Outwardly calm and confident, Patty briefed them on all that had happened, and because of who she was, and because of how valuable *The Great Witchy Cake Off* was to the Witchflix stable, they allowed her to continue the day's filming, saying only that they would review the footage later, and contemplate whether to take action after they had considered the events of the past week or so.

They weren't cancelling the series outright. We took that as a positive sign.

The final three hours of filming passed by in a whirr of weighing and whisking, flouring and frosting, creaming and beating, moulding and icing. Florence whirled around her bench like a dervish, armed with a wooden spoon and a piping bag. I watched her create several layers of cakes, stacking them one on top of another, then carving them into the desired shape. It all looked relatively simple from where I stood, but I knew she'd pull out all of the stops.

And so it transpired.

Mindi counted down the time left until, at last, she issued her final instructions. "Time's up! Hands off your bakes."

To be fair, each contestant had concocted a marvellous creation. Eloise had opted for a large witch's hat decorated with small creatures including a bat, a rat and a spider. Scampi had a large spell book, which he had intricately iced with a spell that, when read aloud, would produce the perfect hot chocolate to complement the cake.

I secretly sniffed in derision.

I didn't need a spell to make the perfect hot chocolate. I had Florence.

Florence proudly accompanied her showstopper as it floated ahead of her, taking up its place on a plinth at the front of the tent where the judges, with Luppitt on camera, awaited her. They cooed at the sight. Florence had carved a large pumpkin carriage cake. Measuring a foot and a half in height, it was a triumph. It bulged the way a fat ripe pumpkin would bulge. Florence had iced it beautifully in an attempt to catch the shades of autumn. She'd carefully crafted sugar glass to create the illuminated windows. Two large black rats, with blue feather plumes cut from coloured rice paper, towed the carriage. But it was the driver I loved the most.

Florence had created an owl, a replica of my own beloved familiar, Mr Hoo. Sporting a smart top hat and tails, his little face and merry orange eyes gazed out at the judges.

"Tell us about your cake, Florence," Faery Kerry instructed Florence.

"Well, this is a homage to my wonderful

employer and friend, Miss Alf, who runs Whittle Inn. She's a brave witch who takes her responsibilities very seriously, but she's kind and compassionate too, although sometimes she can be fierce and a bit grumpy. This is her little friend Mr Hoo. I've created him from a vanilla cake with a caramel frosting. And then the carriage and the rats are made with a dark chocolate cake. The rats have a cappuccino frosting, and the carriage's frosting is flavoured with blood orange. And there's a little surprise when you cut the carriage open."

Raoul wielded his cake knife.

Florence gulped. "Hopefully, anyway."

"Let's have a look, shall we?" Raoul smiled, the familiar twinkle back in his eye, at least for the sake of the camera.

He made two incisions and then pulled a triangle of cake out and placed it carefully on a plate. Luppitt zoomed in a little closer and tightened his focus. Standing behind Ross, who was storing the digital images on his computer, I glanced at the image the camera was picking up. Inside the cake were the shapes of little people, off out for a drive in their pumpkin carriage. Florence had made them from jelly and mousse and then carefully inserted them into the cake when she layered the whole thing together.

Raoul roared his approval. "That's spectacular, Florence. The way you've managed to construct the cake and have these little people inside. Absolutely wonderful. I feel bad about eating them."

"I don't," Faery Kerry said. She forked a whole jelly man into her mouth, and promptly brought the house down.

EPiLOGUE

"It turns out there was DNA on the scarf." George had rung me to fill me in on his latest findings. "Three lots in fact. Janice's, Bertha's and Murgatroyde's. I think Bertha must have gone into the tent after Janice that morning, knowing full well she would make checks on the set as she always did before the start of filming. Janice won't have been unduly alarmed to see Bertha there because it was her job, after all." He paused. "I'm thinking Bertha pulled out the cake knife and Janice panicked and tried to run away. Bertha caught hold of her by the scarf and yanked her back, causing the small friction burn on her neck. When Janice fell to the floor, Bertha stabbed her. Just the once."

"That's all it took." I sighed. Sitting in my office, I leaned back on my chair, pondering on some of the unknowns of the case. "Why keep the scarf though? Some kind of trophy?"

"Maybe, we'll never know, but my guess is that Bertha didn't realise she had a hold of it until she left the marquee. My gut feeling is she was manipulated by her mother to attack Janice. Bertha is no natural murderer. She must have panicked and hidden the scarf. Then, worried it might be found, handed it over to her mother at some later date."

"If Murgatroyde had been a little tidier, I wouldn't have found the scarf," I said. "If her room had been clean, I'd have simply straightened the bed, hoovered and left her to it."

"Silly mistake," George agreed. "We'd probably have shaken Murgatroyde down at some stage—her animosity to Patty has been rumoured over the years —but with your help we arrived there a little faster."

I smiled down the phone. "Always glad to be of service, you know that."

"Is there any chance at all that you and your inn could stay out of trouble from now on?" George asked. "Stop inviting troublesome guests to your inn? Call a truce with The Hay Loft?"

I was suddenly reminded of the predicament I had with Sally McNab-Martin and the rat Crispin Cavendish. At some stage I'd have to tell Millicent, and we'd need to approach Sally carefully. I didn't want to break her heart.

I puffed out my cheeks. "I sincerely doubt it. Trouble is my middle name, apparently." George snorted and I changed the subject. "How's your shoulder?"

"It's fine, thanks to Millicent. I was certain I'd broken a bone somewhere, but the X-ray said not."

"Our lovely Millicent is pretty talented," I confirmed. "In fact—" A knock on the door interrupted my line of thought. "Oh, I have to go, George. I'll speak to you soon, okay?"

"No problem. Take care." He rang off and I stood to open the door. Marissa was on the other side waiting for me.

"I've come to say goodbye," she said.

"You're leaving?" I looked down the hall for Silvan. Wasn't he saying goodbye too?

"I have to get back to London, but I wanted to say thank you for a lovely stay. I've adored every minute, and I've really enjoyed meeting your friends."

"I'm sorry about all the disruptions," I said. "I'd like to say it's not a common occurrence, but I think that would be a lie."

Marissa laughed and reached out to hug me. She

folded me in the lightest of embraces; her form seemed weightless in comparison to mine, her bones so fragile they could have been made of Florence's sugar glass. She smelled sweet, of vanilla and honey, and her gossamer hair brushed my cheek and tickled me. "Tell Silvan goodbye from me too," I said, willing myself not to go and find him and give him the satisfaction of knowing I was thinking of him.

"Oh, he's staying on here for a little while," Marissa said, and pulled back to smile up into my eyes.

"Is he?" *The cheeky oaf.* I wasn't sure whether to feel pleased or irritated. Didn't he know I had an inn-load of new guests due in the morning?

Marissa twinkled. "Oh, Alf, you two do make me laugh. I told you, he talks about you all the time. And when he's not talking about you, he thinks about you."

"Not good thoughts, I'm sure." I tried to cover my embarrassment, but she pursed her lips and gave me a knowing look.

I shook my head in confusion. "But you and he—"

"Are friends. Good friends." She shrugged. "Silvan and I are on markedly different journeys. Our hearts do not beat as one."

I wasn't sure how to process what she seemed to be intimating and couldn't think of how to respond. I studied her for further clues that were not forthcoming.

Instead, she folded her hands around mine once more, squeezing them. "Until we meet again, dear Alf."

The inn was a hive of activity all day.

Outside, the marquee was being dismantled and the equipment stowed away. My lawn beneath the temporary flooring had turned an odd light colour, but with autumn upon us, and with plenty of rain, I knew the grass would soon return to normal.

Inside, Charity was supervising the stripping of beds and cleaning of guest bedrooms, and my Wonky Inn Clean-Up Crew were working flat out to make the inn hospitable for all our new guests due the next day. From downstairs, where order had returned to the kitchen, came the scent of heaven. Monsieur Emietter busily simmered vegetable stock for soups, baked a couple of meat pies, roasted a few chickens and began making cheesecakes to store in the cold room ready for lunch tomorrow.

For my part, I was a little caked out, although I was fairly certain that such a feeling wouldn't last long. Probably until the next time I had a rumbling tummy and a yearning for a cup of tea.

I worked my way through a pile of correspondence, studiously avoiding one particular envelope that had freshly arrived. A fine quality, stained parchment envelope. Cursive handwriting. A foreign stamp.

Sabien.

At twilight, I patted my round belly slightly ruefully. I'd managed no exercise at all since breakfast and couldn't fight a sudden urge to go out for a walk before dinner. I threw my cloak on over my robes and trotted down the front steps. The nights were drawing in and there was a dampness in the air that indicated we were in for a drizzly evening.

Bizarrely, I thought I heard the sound of clucking chickens emanating from somewhere to the rear of the inn, but seeing as I knew we didn't keep chickens, that had to be my imagination.

Right?

I walked in Speckled Wood, as I'd done on many an evening before, but tonight there was something magickal in the air. Tiny sparks of energy lit my way as I trod the ancient path into the forest, my feet instinctively knowing where to tread and how to avoid the roots that might have tripped me or the branches that might catch my hair. On I walked, past the clearing, until I could hear the merry sounds of the Devonshire Fellows, their fingers tripping lightly on strings or tapping the drum in Napier's case with a firm, brash confidence.

I rounded the final bend in the marsh that took me to Vance's pool, and where the last few times I had ducked into the foliage and sunk among the shadows, tonight I had no need. Robert Wait caught my eye and smiled, and Luppitt beckoned me into their circle.

I took a seat on a large boulder at the water's edge, Vance's giant form behind me, swaying gently to the music. Mr Hoo had perched on one of Vance's lower branches and he hoo'd along to the music, every now and then spreading his wings to aid his balance if Vance was a little too adventurous when waving his huge arms around.

Ned had perfected both his dancing and his singing, and now he serenaded a young woman dressed like a milkmaid. I'd never seen her before, but she appeared to be totally smitten with Ned and he with her, for he was solicitous and graceful, and courteous in his advances and beautifully bashful when she—playing at being the reluctant wooee—deigned to address him in return.

I observed this fascinating game of courtship from where I perched on my rock, and I was thrilled for Ned, sure as I could be that he would win his lady love by night's end.

And there were other ghosts joining the party. Gwyn and Zephaniah, my father, and of course the whole of the Wonky Inn Ghostly Clean-Up Crew.

Florence danced with gay abandon. The Witchflix bosses couldn't deny the superiority of her baking prowess and had agreed that the judges could make her runner-up of *The Great Witchy Cake Off*. It aggrieved me that they wouldn't award her the crown, but at the end of the day, the viewers could judge for themselves. My housekeeper hauled a less than enthusiastic Ross on to the makeshift dance floor, where Zephaniah was already jigging with a 1920s flapper. It turned out Ross was a half-decent break-dancer who could spin on his head, but I didn't find that out until much later in the evening, when Elizabethan madrigals gave way to some classic old skool eighties and nineties hip-hop.

I clapped my hands, full of joy to see my friends having such a good time, and when a little later Silvan slipped out of the shadows and joined me, I scooted over on my boulder to give him room. Neither of us said a word for a long while, and for once, neither of us seemed to feel the need to tease the other.

Eventually, I cast a sideways glance at him.

Did Marissa really think he and I were on the same journey? This hardly seemed possible to me. He and I were so different.

Surely?

Silvan continued to look forward, but his lips curled at the corners. He seemed inordinately pleased about something, but all he said, was, "Oh, those green eyes of yours, Alfhild. See how they shine."

You'll have the chance to get your hands on advanced review eBook copies from time to time. I also appreciate your input when I need some help with covers, blurbs etc. We have a giggle.

Or sign up for my newsletter www.subscribepage. com/JeannieWycherleyWonky to keep up to date with what I'm doing next!

WONKY CONTINUES

Vengeful Vampire at Wonky Inn: Wonky Inn Book 8

Vampires are a pain in Alf's neck.

After hosting a diabolical vampire wedding last Halloween, Alf had imagined that Whittle Inn had seen the last of those long-toothed monsters. She'd pointedly barred them from ever setting foot or fang in her part of the English countryside again.

But since then, one thing has continued to bother our favourite wonkiest witch.

Who killed the handsome young vampire, Thaddeus? And why?

Now Alf will have to grit her teeth, because despite her protestations, her undead foes are breathing down her neck and set to make an unwelcome return to her wonky inn. Is anyone safe? How long before another one of their number bites the dust?

Given their previous escapades, Alf and her friends are keen to provide a sharp reality check. But will Sabien and his coven of fiends have the last laugh? Is Alf a match for these bite-young things?

Find out in Vengeful Vampire at Wonky Inn.

A clean and cozy standalone that complements the series as a whole. If you enjoy chaotic and humorous tales of witches, wizards, ghosts, vampires, ents and owls, the Wonky Inn books will cast their spell on you.

Available on Amazon now.

OUT NOW

Dead as a Dodo: A Paranormal Cozy Witch Mystery
(Wonderland Detective Agency Book 1

From the Amazon bestselling author of the Wonky
Inn books comes a brand-new magical fantasy witch
detective series.

Dodo was dead. And there the matter should have
rested.

At least for DS Elise Liddell.

Emotionally burnt out, she considers herself retired
from police work.

By rights it has nothng to do with her, but someone killed the poor man and, as Elise can resist everything except a good puzzle (and a shot of Blue Goblin vodka), here she is tangled up in a murder case.

When a petty thief hands himself into the Ministry of Witches Police Department, Elise's ex-colleagues consider it an open and shut case.

She's less convinced.

Revitalized by the investigation, she takes the suspect on as the first client of her new paranormal detective agency. What would this insignificant wretch have to gain by murdering the cantankerous old wizard? Elise knows full well, by uncovering the motive she can reveal the true killer.

But she forgets, in Tumble Town even the shadows are alive ... and now someone or something is hunting her.

The Wonderland Detective Agency Series is

a paranormal cozy mystery series, set in the same Wonkyverse that readers have already fallen in love with. While some of the characters and places will be instantly familiar, Wycherley effortlessly casts her spell so that her zany new friends quickly become ours too.

Packed full of witches, wizards, warlocks, ghosts, shadow people and more, you'll love this glimpse into the dark side.
Take a walk in Tumble Town today!

THE WONKY INN SERIES

The Complete Wonky Inn Series (in chronological reading order)

The Wonkiest Witch: Wonky Inn Book 1

The Ghosts of Wonky Inn: Wonky Inn Book 2

Weird Wedding at Wonky Inn: Wonky Inn Book 3

The Witch Who Killed Christmas: Wonky Inn Christmas Special

Fearful Fortunes and Terrible Tarot: Wonky Inn Book 4

The Mystery of the Marsh Malaise: Wonky Inn Book 5

The Mysterious Mr Wylie: Wonky Inn Book 6

The Great Witchy Cake Off: Wonky Inn Book 7

Vengeful Vampire at Wonky Inn: Wonky Inn Book 8

Witching in a Winter Wonkyland: A Wonky Inn Christmas Cozy Special

A Gaggle of Ghastly Grandmamas: Wonky Inn
Book 9

Magic, Murder and a Movie Star: Wonky Inn
Book 10

O' Witchy Town of Whittlecombe: A Wonky Inn
Christmas Cozy Special

Judge, Jury and Jailhouse Rockcakes: Wonky Inn
Book 11

A Midsummer Night's Wonky: Wonky Inn Book 12

Halloween Heebie-Geebies: Wonky Inn Book 13

Owl I want for Witchmas is Hoo: A Wonky Inn
Christmas Cozy Mystery (Release Date October
2021)

Oh Mummy!: Wonky Inn Book 14 (Release Date
2022 TBC)

ALSO BY

Spellbound Hound

Ain't Nothing but a Pound Dog: Spellbound Hound Magic and Mystery Book 1

A Curse, a Coven and a Canine: Spellbound Hound Magic and Mystery Book 2

Bark Side of the Moon: Spellbound Hound Magic and Mystery Book 3

Master of Puppies: Spellbound Hound Magic and Mystery Book 4 (2022 TBC)

Wonderland Detective Agency

Dead as a Dodo: Wonderland Detective Agency Book 1

The Rabbit Hole Murders: Wonderland Detective Agency Book 2

Tweedledumb and Tweedledie: Wonderland Detective Agency Book 3

The Curious Incident at the Pig and Pepper: Wonderland Detective Agency Book 4 (2022 TBC)

Also by Jeannie Wycherley

The Municipality of Lost Souls (2020)

Midnight Garden: The Extra Ordinary World Novella Series Book 1 (2019)

Beyond the Veil

Crone

A Concerto for the Dead and Dying

Deadly Encounters: A collection of short stories

Keepers of the Flame: A love story

Non-Fiction

Losing my best Friend: Thoughtful support for those affected by dog bereavement or pet loss

Follow Jeannie Wycherley

Find out more at on the website

www.jeanniewycherley.co.uk

You can tweet Jeannie

twitter.com/Thecushionlady

Or visit her on Facebook for her fiction

www.facebook.com/jeanniewycherley

Follow Jeannie on Instagram (for bears and books)

www.instagram.com/jeanniewycherley

Sign up for Jeannie's newsletter on her website

www.subscribepage.com/JeannieWycherleyWonky

Made in the USA
Middletown, DE
09 November 2022

14447136R00194